Her lips…her full, trembling lips…tempted him. He leaned his weight against her and felt her body respond. Was that only to him? He pulled back again and stared down at her. She met his gaze levelly, and this time there were no tears.

'I want you,' she murmured, and her eyes had grown dark and slumberous. Brushing her hair back from her brow, as if he would find something to steal his trust away beneath its silky weight, he dipped his head and kissed her.

It felt like coming home.

He had to remind himself he had many homes and didn't stay long in any of them.

Susan Stephens was a professional singer before meeting her husband on the tiny Mediterranean island of Malta. In true Modern™ Romance style they met on Monday, became engaged on Friday and were married three months after that. Almost thirty years and three children later, they are still in love. (Susan does not advise her children to return home one day with a similar story, as she may not take the news with the same fortitude as her own mother!)

Susan had written several non-fiction books when fate took a hand. At a charity costume ball there was an after-dinner auction. One of the lots, 'Spend a Day with an Author', had been donated by Mills & Boon® author Penny Jordan. Susan's husband bought this lot, and Penny was to become not just a great friend but a wonderful mentor, who encouraged Susan to write romance.

Susan loves her family, her pets, her friends and her writing. She enjoys entertaining, travel and going to the theatre. She reads, cooks, and plays the piano to relax, and can occasionally be found throwing herself off mountains on a pair of skis or galloping through the countryside. Visit Susan's website: www.susanstephens.net—she loves to hear from her readers all around the world!

Recent books by the same author:

COUNT MAXIME'S VIRGIN

BY
SUSAN STEPHENS

MILLS & BOON™
Pure reading pleasure™

All the characters in this book have no existence outside the imagination of the author, and have no relation whatsoever to anyone bearing the same name or names. They are not even distantly inspired by any individual known or unknown to the author, and all the incidents are pure invention.

First published in Great Britain 2008
Paperback edition 2009
Harlequin Mills & Boon Limited,
Eton House, 18-24 Paradise Road, Richmond, Surrey TW9 1SR

© Susan Stephens 2008

ISBN: 978 0 263 87001 5

Set in Times Roman 10½ on 12¼ pt
01-0209-47797

Printed and bound in Spain
by Litografia Rosés, S.A., Barcelona

COUNT MAXIME'S VIRGIN

*For my friends, Danielle and Cathy,
and of course for la belle France.*

CHAPTER ONE

THE men in the bar of the fancy London hotel had laughingly agreed that Tara should get out more. The better-looking of the two, a tall, powerfully built man called Lucien, with striking dark looks and thick nut-brown hair, argued with Tara's older sister, Freya, that there was no such thing as 'too quiet', and if Tara didn't want to party hard, why should she? Having flashed him a grateful glance, Tara sank back into the shadows with relief.

To get close to her sister was all eighteen-year-old Tara had ever wanted, but she was beginning to wonder if it was possible to get close to a flame that burned as bright as Freya. Maybe this was the way, Tara reflected later as she squeezed into some of her sister's clothes. The two girls had returned to their bedsit alone and were preparing to go out with the men they'd met earlier. Freya was always encouraging Tara to socialise, and tonight Tara felt it was a chance for her to prove she would do pretty much anything to win Freya's approval.

But not *that*, Tara thought, as the face of the man who had defended her earlier swam into her mind. Lucien's dark chocolate voice and black amused gaze had made her feel so nervous. He belonged to that other, more exciting world, the world Freya yearned to inhabit, the world in which Tara knew she didn't fit.

Freya thought nothing of talking to men they didn't know, but it was agony for Tara, who had hardly raised her eyes during the whole embarrassing encounter. She had felt so tongue-tied and gauche, so fat and so plain in her charity shop clothes, perched next to a glamorous older sister who drew attention wherever she went. She had wanted to disappear, and had only looked up once more when she'd been forced to answer the Lucien's direct question: 'Shouldn't you be studying?'

Instead of picking up men in a bar, she had presumed he meant. She had told him she did study, but by then, of course, Freya had moved the conversation on, wanting nothing to detract from the flirtatious tone she'd set. When Tara mentioned the remark later, Freya had laughed it off, saying Tara mustn't let it get to her, and that she had the rest of her life to study, and must use her youth to snare a man…

Tara's face was burning with humiliation as she thought about this now, though in fairness Freya had been partly right, for whatever he'd said about studying, Lucien, with the exotic accent, whose knowing gaze had sent flames of heat pulsing through her secret places, had asked Freya to make sure her little sister accompanied her to the party tonight.

Why had he done that? Tara wondered, going hot and cold as she thought about it. She already felt ridiculous, sitting here in their draughty bedsit, drenched in Freya's French perfume and wearing a body control underskirt Freya had said she must to create the right first impression. The second impression didn't bear thinking about. She'd have to be cut out of this top, just for starters.

'Stop fiddling with that top, Tara,' Freya insisted, breaking off from skilfully applying false eyelashes to admonish her. 'It cost a fortune—'

'Sorry…' Freya had insisted she must wear something glamorous tonight, and had pushed the spangled top into her hands. She was about to stop fiddling as instructed when Freya snatched it back.

'I've decided to wear it. You can have this one—'

'Thank you…' It was such a relief to exchange the glittery top Freya had picked out for her to wear, for an older, duller boob tube with a much more modest neckline.

'I hope you know your man's a count?' Freya pouted in the mirror as she applied her lip gloss.

'A count?' Tara's heart rate doubled. 'Really?' No wonder Lucien, the man who made her pulse race, was so confident and commanding. But since when was he *her* man? And if he was *her* man, what on earth was she supposed to do with him, never mind the fact that he was a count! She would never think of a thing to say to interest a man like that.

'You're a very lucky girl. It's up to you to make the most of tonight. Who knows…?'

Who knew what? Tara wondered, struggling to heave the Freya-sized Lycra top over her head. She raised a hesitant smile to please her sister. One thing was sure, she didn't know *anything* about *that* stuff, although her determination to better herself was no less than Freya's. There might not be room for a desk in their tiny room, but the books she was studying were kept safely under the bed.

'Here, put this wrap on—' Freya tossed what looked like a fabulous genuine fur in her direction.

'I'd rather not—' Tara shrank from the deep white pelt. In her imagination it still carried the faint scent of fresh air and freedom.

'Why ever not?' Freya demanded impatiently.

'I might spill something on it—' She hoped Freya was convinced by her excuse.

'Oh, all right then.' Freya pulled a face as she sorted through the tumble of clothes on her side of the bed. 'Take this shawl instead.'

Tara thought the pale blue shawl much prettier than the fur. Stroking it appreciatively, she thought about Freya's explanation for this fabulous collection of expensive things. 'Men like to buy me presents,' Freya had said, 'and what's wrong with that?' Nothing, Tara thought now, smiling fondly at her beautiful sister. Who wouldn't want to buy Freya gifts? When you lived like this and looked like Freya, no wonder her poor sister yearned for something better.

'What's that sigh for?' Freya demanded suspiciously as Tara started clearing up Freya's discarded tissues.

'Nothing…' Realising Freya had thought her sigh a complaint, Tara rushed to lay out her sister's coat and bag.

'See to yourself,' Freya snapped. 'I left that skirt out for you specially. Come on, Tara,' she chivvied as Tara viewed the tight skirt dubiously, 'we mustn't be late. And you can leave those cushions,' Freya snapped, bringing Tara to a standstill. 'They don't need plumping. I don't know why you bought them in the first place. No one's going to see them. For goodness' sake, stop tidying the room. You'll get all hot and bothered and we don't want that.'

What Freya did want from tonight made Tara very nervous. She knew she was destined to be a failure, because Lucien wasn't interested in her, and anything nice he'd said was just him being kind. That hadn't stopped her daydreams, which had a very dark edge to them, for they contained a lot of kissing and touching, which she knew was wrong.

She wasted some precious time fighting with the back zip on the skirt Freya had lent her, which was at least two sizes too small. In the end, she was forced to give up. Flashing a guilty glance at Freya, who thankfully hadn't noticed, she left the skirt open an inch or two at the top and folded the fabric over.

'Ready?' Freya demanded, snatching up her smart new red patent bag.

Ready to try not to show Freya up, Tara thought anxiously, straightening her tights. She hoped she could manage that much.

'Damn, it's so cold in here,' Freya said, rubbing her arms briskly. 'Come on, it's probably several degrees warmer outside.'

'If your fingers weren't half frozen you'd have been ready ages ago,' Tara said, laughing nervously in an attempt to cheer up her sister. She so loved to see Freya smile, but Freya was tense tonight, and Tara didn't need her sister to tell her that a lot hung on the outcome of their meeting with the two men.

Freya soon confirmed these thoughts. 'Don't worry, little sister; I don't plan to be living here much longer.'

Tara blinked at the horror of being separated from Freya. 'What do you mean?'

'I mean there's a big, wide world out there with a lot of wealthy men inhabiting it, men who want a woman just like me.'

'Oh…' Tara bit her bottom lip nervously. Of course

Freya deserved a better future, but as her own future rose like an empty canvas in front of her Tara wondered if she would ever get over being separated from her sister. They were orphans and Freya was the only family she had.

'You can always stay on here,' Freya said, continuing to touch up her hair as she spoke. 'Well, it's a start for you, isn't it?' she added, glancing at Tara. 'I'll sign the lease over to you before I go, as, most likely, I'll be living in the south of France—'

Tara knew it was the life her beautiful sister deserved, even if it left her feeling hollow inside. She brushed these selfish thoughts away. 'You always think of me.' She smiled, getting off the bed to give Freya a hug.

'Mind my make up,' Freya warned, backing away hastily. 'Now, listen to me,' she began firmly. 'You must make sure that count of yours takes you to his place tonight. He mustn't see this dump—'

'He isn't *my* Count,' Tara ventured, 'and I definitely won't be going home with him—'

'I wouldn't be so sure about that.' Freya turned and studied Tara keenly. 'You might be overweight, but you clean up well…'

'Not as well as you…'

'Ah, well…' Freya sighed with satisfaction as she took one last look at herself in the mirror. 'Hurry, hurry, hurry,' she exclaimed, spinning on her five-inch heels. 'We can't risk anyone poaching our men…'

He was restless as he waited for the two girls to arrive. This outing was a first for him. He never accompanied his brother, Guy, on his hunting expeditions, and yet here he was in a high-class pick-up joint, which his brother had persuaded him was the 'in' place that season.

SUSAN STEPHENS

13

After the encounter with the two women that afternoon he hadn't been able to shake the image of a timid
young girl who had wanted to disappear into the
shadows. And would have done if he hadn't coaxed her
out of them, he remembered, flashing a glance at his
watch, wondering what was keeping Tara. An occasion
he had been so sure would bore him had acquired
piquancy, thanks to her. Tara Devenish must be at least
ten years younger than he was, Lucien reflected, though
her sister's colourful reputation suggested Tara was no
innocent. His body warmed at that thought, and right on
cue the door of the exclusive supper club opened and in
she walked.

The Count of Ferranbeaux drew the attention of the
whole room as he rose to his feet. People sensed the
dangerous edge to Lucien's mature elegance and it
stopped conversation dead. Lucien was accepting of his
physical needs, and after a week of non-stop business
meetings even he would have admitted that his libido was
in the danger zone, though he could not know that the
miasma of testosterone cloaking his muscular frame was
almost palpable.

Lucien made a silent note to add a London home to
his ever-growing property portfolio. Entertaining in
nightclubs wasn't for him, especially not on an evening
like this. Tara was even lovelier than he remembered.
She was quirkier and a good deal more outlandishly
dressed too. Her pencil skirt had clearly been borrowed
from her much slimmer sister, and the way she'd been
forced to hitch it up had left it a good four inches short
of respectable. Her ample breasts were stuffed for the
occasion into a tight boob tube that revealed some
tempting pale flesh, which for some reason she was

trying to cover with a pale blue shawl. Surely, his cynical self calculated, shouldn't she be putting her wares on view rather than hiding them away?

He noticed nothing other than Tara as she walked towards him. He felt her aura of innocence, fear and excitement sweep over him, and when she stopped in front of him and gazed up tremulously he reached for her hand. Bowing over it, he raised it to his lips and, as her gaze sought his face, he felt her tremble.

The evening passed in a blur. The Count was at least ten times more attractive and a good deal more worldly-wise than Tara had remembered. Dressed in an impeccable dinner suit with a crisp white shirt, highly polished shoes and fine black socks, he looked like a film star and couldn't have attracted more attention from all the ladies present had he tried.

Which he didn't, and that was one of the nicest things about him. Even nicer than that was the way he looked after her. It was a little unnerving to begin with, because he was so much older than she was and her imagination insisted on working overtime, conjuring up all sorts of forbidden possibilities, but somehow he managed to make her relax. Then it was like a fairy tale. In her dreams she had always favoured the dark, flashing Latin looks of a Mediterranean hero, and Lucien Maxime, the Count of Ferranbeaux, or Lucien, as he had insisted she must call him, took Latin to the extreme.

As he turned to order another bottle of champagne, she stole a proper look at him. Lucien was very tall and very tanned, with hair the colour of roast chestnuts. It was thick and wavy, glossy hair, which he wore a little long, and as the evening progressed Tara decided that with the rough black stubble on Lucien's face, combined with those dark flashing eyes, he looked like a dangerous pirate. A pirate dressed by Savile Row, of course.

'Are you all right?' Lucien enquired, sensing her interest.

Better than all right. But as the keen black stare remained fixed on her face she went all wobbly inside and quickly folded her hands primly in her lap. 'Yes, thank you,' she replied politely.

Her simple remark prompted the wickedest look, as if Lucien knew her innocent pose covered some very naughty undercurrents and she gasped as his hand covered hers, though it was barely there for a moment. When he took his hand away she gazed down, certain his print would be branded there. She remained quite still after that, hardly able to believe the Count of Ferranbeaux had actually touched her. Then Freya said something and the spell was broken as Lucien turned away to take part in Guy and Freya's far livelier conversation, leaving her to watch his sensual lips move as he spoke, and dream more dreams as she inhaled his fabulous cologne.

How was she to guess he would turn so quickly and catch her looking at him? It was a relief when he said nothing to embarrass her, but, as one of his ebony brows peaked, she guessed he knew exactly what she'd been thinking.

Turning away to hide her burning face, Tara retreated into her thoughts, where she could have the luxury of the most frenzied fantasies. The conversation buzzed around her, but she was oblivious to it. She was too busy revelling in a fantasy world where a much older man was about to introduce a young, untried girl to a range of forbidden pleasures.

Freya's voice jerked her rudely out of this happy state. 'Come on, Tara, drink up,' she insisted impatiently.

Tara's cheeks flamed red as everyone turned to look at her. She had been trying so hard to keep up with Freya's drinking, for fear of being ridiculed, but had failed miserably. She had resorted to pouring her champagne into a conveniently placed plant pot when no one was looking, but now had no alternative other than to drain her glass.

Taking her by surprise, Lucien lifted it from her hand. 'We shouldn't kill too many plants,' he murmured discreetly, drinking it down, 'or they might not let us come here again—'

'Would that upset you?' Tara exclaimed, instantly concerned that she had offended him.

'Not a bit,' he confided, leaning close so that her face tingled with his warmth.

Of course he pulled away again, but not before she had felt a glow of happiness at sharing this private moment with him. She knew it was going nowhere, but made an extra effort to look good when he turned away. She smoothed her skirt and tried to tug it down to appear respectable, but it was Freya's and Freya liked to wear her skirts short. Adjusting her position on the banquette, Tara tried again. It was suddenly very important to her that Lucien shouldn't be ashamed of being seen with her. He was so elegant and she already liked him far too much to show him up.

She mustn't let these daydreams get out of hand, Tara's sensible inner voice warned. It was clear to everyone that Lucien Maxime was only trying to make her feel at ease and would barely register her existence by tomorrow.

Realising her restlessness had caused a pause in the conversation, Tara listened to her own good advice and remained very still. It would suit her best to be invisible for the rest of the evening, she decided.

They moved on to a restaurant, where Tara watched closely to make sure she was using the correct cutlery for each course. Lucien was kind again, arranging her napkin and spreading paté on her toast when she had been about to attack it with a knife and fork. She reached for some more bread, but quickly withdrew her hand when Freya gave her a warning look. They had agreed that Tara mustn't put on any more weight.

'You haven't finished your meal, I hope?' Lucien smiled at her as she scrunched her napkin anxiously. 'Here, try this… No…? A spear of asparagus won't hurt you.'

Asparagus with butter dripping from it? Tara shook her head a second time, but Lucien insisted on feeding the succulent spear to her himself, even mopping her chin with his own napkin when butter smeared her lips. And, as if that wasn't bad enough, he blotted some of the juice with his thumb sucking it whilst holding her gaze. This had an alarming effect on her, coaxing endless little pleasure pulses out of those secret places she wanted him to touch. Deciding a man like Lucien would surely know that made her cheeks fire up again. If there was a more sensual message a man could deliver to a woman, Tara couldn't imagine what it might be. But how she was supposed to respond to such advances remained a mystery to her.

She must be joined to Lucien by some invisible chain, Tara decided as her gaze kept wandering to him. Perhaps she was bewitched by him for, rather than wishing the evening could be over with, or that she could be invisible, she wanted the night to last for ever.

Freya soon put a stop to that, announcing that it was time to move on to an all night jazz club.

'Don't look so worried,' Lucien reassured Tara, seeing how concerned she was. 'You're coming home with me…'

Tara's face lit up. She was so grateful to Lucien. An early night, safe and alone with her dreams, was exactly what she wanted.

CHAPTER TWO

TARA was so relieved to hear that Lucien was taking her home she relaxed immediately and threw him a grateful glance. Then she saw how delighted Freya was and realised she'd missed the meaning behind Lucien's message. Going home with him meant going back to his hotel room.

She felt such a fool when they arrived outside the grand entrance to Lucien's magnificent penthouse suite, and only fear of upsetting Freya prompted her to follow him inside. Freya's insistent whispering before they'd parted—that everything was going so well for her and Guy that Tara mustn't screw things up now—was ringing in her head. Her fate was sealed, Tara realised the moment Lucien closed the door, for if there was an eighteen-year-old who could resist the Count of Ferranbeaux's brutally masculine charm it wasn't her.

She stepped cautiously across a cream-coloured carpet with pile so deep it felt like a mattress and gazed in awe at antique mirrors framed in gold, and at grand vases in matching pairs as tall as she was. The furniture was antique and both fabrics and walls were decorated in ivory and cream, as if dirt wouldn't dare to intrude here. The ceilings were high and decorated with gilt and plasterwork, and there was a heady fragrance in the air which she couldn't place at first, and then she realised it was wealth.

She was so entranced that Lucien had to take her by the elbow and lead her into the next room. This room was equally ornate, with arched windows dressed in heavy soft gold silk and a fire burning silently behind a glass screen.

'It's fake,' Lucien murmured, seeing her staring at the fire.

Of course she knew that, Tara pretended, reddening as she gave a little self-conscious laugh. It was a gas flame fire; she could see that now. She turned away quickly, though how she was supposed to act nonchalant amidst all this luxury, she had had no idea. She was standing in the middle of an intimate sitting room of a type she had no idea existed in hotels. It was a home away from home for the super-rich, she surmised, with magazines on the table, books on the shelves and an assortment of fruit that looked as if it had been picked that very morning. There were pictures on the walls that might have been original works of art and, instead of wallpaper, fabric—silk—glowing softly in tones of rich bronze and…

'Come over here and sit down before you fall over,' Lucien prompted.

She turned to see him smiling at her. What a country bumpkin he must think her. She pulled herself together quickly and crossed the room, trying to look confident, but there were so many lamps and tables she hardly knew where to tread and, in her usual clumsy way, she managed to stumble over a chair leg. Gasping with alarm, she reached out, only to feel strong arms catching her.

'Better now?' Lucien commented good-naturedly, steadying her back on her feet.

She had felt so safe in his arms that perhaps she didn't move as quickly as she ought to have done, and his next words proved it. 'I was going to order champagne,' he murmured against her hair, 'but I've changed my mind…'

She stared up at him, and his knowing half-smile sent ribbons of seduction rippling through her. She closed her eyes and just for a moment allowed herself to believe he was as captivated by her as she was by him and that now was the moment when he would sweep her off her feet…

'I've some freshly squeezed orange juice in the fridge,' he said casually, setting her aside so he could move towards the smart built-in bar. 'Or perhaps you would prefer me to call down for a hot drink…' He turned at this point. 'Cocoa, perhaps?'

Cocoa? Freya would not be pleased. Tara gulped unhappily. She could think of nothing to say. But how would she ever explain this mess to Freya?

'Why don't I make myself comfortable,' Lucien suggested, 'while you make up your mind?'

He was doing everything he could to make this easy for her, Tara realised, but she still couldn't relax. Her throat felt so dry she couldn't have spoken a word to him even if she could have thought of something to say. One look from Lucien was all it took to make her nipples pucker, so she crossed her arms over her chest and remained where she was, dithering in the middle of the room.

Lucien shrugged off his jacket, and his look of amusement caught her mid-gulp as she weighed up the width of his shoulders. She turned away, but not before registering the fact that his fingers were supple and capable as he deftly untied his bow-tie, and this only stirred more rebellion in her lower regions, which she could have well done without. Leaving the tie hanging, he next freed some buttons at the neck of his shirt. Sneaking glances at him, she now decided he looked exactly like a man in an advertisement for some high end luxury product, though far more handsome, of course. She went all dreamy again as she imagined touching that smooth tanned flesh and feeling it warm beneath her hands until the jangle of Lucien's heavy gold cuff-links hitting a glass bowl on the table jerked her back to reality.

'Won't you at least take your shawl off?' Lucien encouraged. 'Here, I'll put it somewhere safe for you…' He held out his hand.

She stared at him foolishly. By now he was folding back his sleeves, revealing powerful forearms shaded with black hair. 'I was just about to take it off,' she lied, wondering how a single inch of Lucien's fabulous suite could be called safe while he was in it. She took off her shawl, conscious that an acre of untoned naked flesh was now on show. Freya's hours at the gym had paid dividends for her, but Tara didn't have the time between jobs to follow suit, and would have felt too embarrassed to strip down in front of everyone, anyway.

'Come and sit here with me,' Lucien invited, beckoning her over to one of the sofas.

She chose the couch facing his and perched tensely on the edge of it. She was careful to sit very straight and lift her ribcage as Freya had shown her, in order to prevent herself looking too plump. But, as she did so, Lucien murmured, 'Impressive…'

Did he mean to give her confidence? She gulped in

horror, realising too late that he must think she was displaying her breasts for his approval. She quickly hunched her shoulders and lowered her gaze.

'Do I make you so nervous, *ma petite*?'

Risking a glance at him, she garbled something unintelligible that made him laugh.

'I don't think I am succeeding at putting you at your ease, am I?' Lucien demanded softly, 'though I'd very much like to do so…'

By sitting next to her? By draping his arm across her shoulders? She was about as far from at ease as she had ever been. In fact, she was quivering all over, wondering what Lucien expected of her.

'Relax,' he murmured, making her ear tingle with his warm, minty breath.

There was something so soothing in his voice she leaned into him. It felt so good just for a moment to rest her head against his firm chest and listen to the steady beat of his heart. Lucien made her feel so secure, and just for once she longed for rock instead of shifting sand, but when he brushed some errant strands of hair from her brow with his lips, she stirred self-consciously. 'Relax,' Lucien insisted.

She tried so hard to do what he wanted, but all the time her inner voice was warning her that this was no dream and was far more reality than she could handle.

'What would you like me to do next, little one?' Lucien murmured.

Her gaze flickered up, only to discover that Lucien's had darkened from sepia to black. Did that mean the world of wicked thoughts in her head was an open book to him? His knowing look suggested that was exactly the case, and his next words confirmed it. 'Shall we go to the bedroom?'

As he spoke Lucien touched his forehead to hers. It was such an intimate thing to do, her dreams took flight again. Oh, yes, she wanted to say, let's go there now, but she heard herself reply, 'I'm quite comfortable here, thank you.' Her voice had grown very small, and she knew that at this point she was supposed to sound breathy and provocative, as Freya had taught her.

'Then we'll stay here,' Lucien agreed with a shrug.

He didn't seem the least bit disappointed in her, Tara noticed with relief.

'Don't look so worried,' he insisted, cupping her chin. 'I won't bite…'

Or, at least, if he did, she would enjoy it, Tara thought as Lucien's lips tugged in a wicked half-smile. Sensation streamed through her at this thought, which he must have sensed because the hand that wasn't caressing her jaw began trailing a path of fire down her neck to her breastbone and, from there, unbelievably, incredibly, and quite fantastically, on to her bosom. She was transfixed. Whatever she had imagined about sensation, this was so much more—so much better. She hardly dared to breathe in case she distracted him as Lucien's sensitive fingers continued to tease and coax and cajole. Smiling faintly whilst holding her gaze, he murmured something in his own language. She didn't know what he said, but she could imagine and it made her groan.

'I think you like that,' he observed, continuing to abrade the tip of her nipple.

So much, he could have no idea. No one had ever touched her there before, and she doubted anyone could have coaxed so much feeling out of her. And yes, she liked it; she liked it a lot. Added to which, Lucien's stern voice was strumming her senses and causing the ache between her legs to grow until she could hardly remain still.

'You do like that,' he approved as she groaned once more beneath his skilful touches. She wouldn't know where to begin telling him how much. Her breathing was fast and shallow and her eyes were locked onto his burning gaze. She had no idea how to put her thoughts, her needs into words, though she was desperate to communicate them to him. Her biggest fear was that Lucien would tire of this and let her go. Unsure as she was of their final destination, she wanted to experience everything Lucien could teach her along the way. She was grateful when the flimsy top she'd had so much trouble tugging on proved no barrier to Lucien's explorations. He drew it over her head quite easily and then stared openly at her naked breasts, making a sound with his tongue against his teeth and shaking his head in disapproval when she tried to cover them.

'You should wear a bra,' he said at last.

'Should I?' she said anxiously, even as his stern command sent a pulse of arousal darting to her core. Something else she'd got wrong.

'Of course you should,' Lucien murmured with amusement, 'because that way there'd be more layers for me to unwrap, and I enjoy the process...'

She was beginning to understand the game, Tara realised, risking an uncertain laugh as Lucien peeled off her skirt.

'You must never, *never* apologise,' Lucien insisted. 'Certainly not for your magnificent breasts.'

He weighed them appreciatively in his big hands as he said this and, rolling her head back, she sighed, thrusting them towards him for more of his delicious attention.

She wanted as much of this as Lucien had to give her, but the moment he turned away to reach for something in a drawer she took the opportunity to tug off her shabby knickers. Lingerie was the one thing she had put her foot down over. Freya had wanted her to wear an uncomfortable lacy thong, while she preferred her tried and trusted comfortable knickers. But they were very old now, and she couldn't bear for Lucien to see them. By the time he turned back to her she had rolled them up in her discarded skirt.

Dipping his head, Lucien buried his face in her cleavage before rasping his stubble against her super-sensitised skin, and by the time he tugged on her nipples again she could only cry out with abandonment. 'Oh, Lucien, I can't bear this…'

'Can't bear what?' he demanded sternly. 'This?' He suckled fiercely on one nipple, teasing the other between his thumb and forefinger. 'Or this…?' His voice was firmer still as he slipped a hand between her thighs, teasing the silky curls.

'Both,' she cried out in a voice that begged him for more. 'I can't choose… I don't know…'

By this time she was crazy for him and squirmed shamelessly beneath his touch. She had no idea how to ease the frustration mounting inside her, and only knew that she must… 'No!' she cried wildly when Lucien stopped touching her.

Lifting his handsome head, he studied the effect he was having on her with slumberous intent. 'No?' murmured.

'No, don't stop!' she explained frantically. Burying her fingers in his thick hair, she brought him back to her. Nothing—*nothing*—must stop this feeling inside her… *It* was going somewhere wonderful, though she didn't know where. Lucien had awoken appetites she had never guessed she had, and these appetites were sucking out the common sense from her head and replacing it with hot, hungry need.

He had anticipated her skin was like silk that carried the faint aroma of summer meadows, but he had not expected his fingertips to tingle with awareness like this. He took his time to trace each smooth pale inch of her, marvelling as he did so at the way her breasts filled his palms as if they had been made to fit there. Wherever he touched made her groan with pleasure, and whenever she groaned he found some new place to explore and increase that pleasure. Long before he had been ready to undress her she had started wriggling out of her wretched skirt, and he'd only had to help her to remove it. When he'd turned back to her after securing protection for them both, she had attacked his shirt without any of her former timidity, tugging it out of the waistband of his trousers and pushing it from his shoulders with a gasp of admiration. He wasn't a vain man, but he had always made time to work out. As she whimpered and reached for him, he realised he had never known a woman so hungry for love before. She was moving and clutching and sighing and even parting her thighs for him before he had thought of preparing her. 'Not so fast,' he warned. 'You'll enjoy it so much more if you learn to take your time…'

He had intended this to be a lingering seduction, but it seemed to him that Tara's intentions were very different. Perhaps she had been instructed to snare him fast? Perhaps those were her orders from her sister, Freya? Freya had hinted as much to him with her knowing looks and lascivious smiles in the direction of her younger sister, though if he had sensed Tara was at all unwilling he would have acted quite differently. Reluctantly, he was coming to the conclusion that Tara was part of a sophisticated double act in which she played as crucial a role in padding out the family finances as her sister.

There was an upside to this. It gave him the freedom to enjoy her, and he would make it worth her while. He was disappointed in her, he couldn't deny it, but the thought of sinking into that moist, plump flesh…the thought of pleasuring her, was irresistible.

But he would not make Guy's mistake and imagine this was more than it was.

'Lucien?'

He was instantly distracted by a voice as sweet and as innocent as Freya could have wished for. 'What is it, *ma petite*?' He had to hand it to Freya—she had trained her sister well. 'Tell me, *chérie*,' he encouraged. Tara was still new enough at this for him to want to take care of her.

She pouted prettily, a device no doubt learned from her sister. Tara might lack Freya's polished skills, but that didn't stop her throwing everything she had into this pursuit of her wealthy target. 'You have forgotten me, Lucien,' she complained.

'Never,' he murmured, soothing and petting her. But it wasn't enough; she wanted more. Of course she did. She had been told she must return to Freya like a hunter with her prize of a wealthy lover in the bag.

Even at the age of eighteen and a virgin, Tara knew the danger signals and had chosen to ignore them. She believed this was her one and only chance to live the fairy tale and have an incredible-looking man like Lucien Maxime make love to her. But, more importantly, she felt safe with him, and she had never felt safe before. In his eyes she could see the reflection of a sophisticated, smooth-running world where everyone was safe. She longed to be part of that world, under Lucien's protection, and knew she never could be, though for this one night she could pretend...

At the touch of his fingertips on her naked arms she exhaled raggedly. Lucien could communicate so much through touch. He promised so much pleasure, and she wanted to experience that pleasure. She wriggled shamelessly into a position where his hand must encounter her breast again. She might be plain, but she had seen men look at her chest before, and knew they liked it... If she could just keep Lucien's thoughts on the pleasures her body could afford him, perhaps he wouldn't turn away just yet...

She was perfect. Her breasts were a feast of perfection and he thought her lovely. This might be going nowhere, but he could lose himself for now. Tara was doing everything she could to make this possible for him and in return he would take her to paradise and back. If there was one thing he understood about a woman, it was her body and how to make it sing.

He lavished attention on every smooth and perfect inch of her, kissing and caressing her as he made her wait so that her senses sharpened. When that moment came and she couldn't wait any longer she grabbed his hand, guiding him to the sweet swell of her belly and pushing his hand down between her legs again. She parted those legs as if it was the most natural thing on earth to her, and even lifted her knees to encourage his exploration.

Moving down the bed, he tasted her and found her more than ready, but it pleased him to hold her back a little longer, knowing her pleasure would increase if she would only wait. She called to him during all this time with little whimpers of desire, which he answered by parting those swollen lips to find the receptive little bud trembling in anticipation of his touch. At the first lash of his tongue she shrieked his name. He caught her as she bucked and held her firmly in place to make sure she derived maximum pleasure from the experience. Far from subsiding in his arms when it was over, she clung to him and begged for more.

'Of course, *ma petite*...' He reasoned that she would want him to go 'all the way' so she could report back to Freya that she had bagged the Count as instructed. And she had, he thought a little sadly, knowing he was being manipulated. With his appetite, it was hardly likely that one night of excess with such a voluptuous young woman would be enough for him. His only hope of salvation was that by morning he would wake to find reason had returned.

Having protected them both, he slipped a pillow beneath her hips to tilt her into the most receptive position. Moving over her, he paused. The anticipation of sinking into that warm, throbbing flesh was so intense he wanted to hold back and savour the moment, but she wouldn't have it and, drawing up her knees as far as she could, she looked at him plaintively. He feasted his gaze on somewhere other than her face before testing himself inside her. They both exhaled sharply, which told him that neither of them could possibly have predicted this level of sensation. Even with his experience, this was a revelation. He withdrew completely, only in order to enjoy entering her again. He went deeper this time, taking her slowly and gently, conscious that he was stretching her. Whatever he thought of her, and whatever her level of experience, he was so much stronger than she was and honour demanded that he must treat her with care. When he thought he might be hurting her he stopped, but she urged him on, clamping her fingertips into his buttocks and working with him.

'Please Lucien…don't stop now,' she begged him when his impulse was to soothe her. But she was very tight, and he was very large, which made him move with the utmost care. Finally it seemed she relaxed again, and as her pleasure built her mouth fell open, and it pleased him to hear her sob in ecstasy.

He could see she was consumed by pleasure as he set up a regular pattern. He stared deep into her eyes to ensure she enjoyed this on every level. Her answer was to urge him on, straining to meet every stroke he dealt her as she closed her muscles around him to draw him deep.

It was more important for him to please Tara than he could possibly have imagined, though the sane part of his brain continued to warn that she had been well trained to please a man. He could see it all now. The Devenish sisters had set out that night in a wholly calculated manner to land a double prize, but whereas Freya might have succeeded, Tara's future remained in her own hands.

She lay next to him, watching Lucien sleep. The fantasy might be over, but she was determined to imprint every fragment of it on her mind. Biting down on her lip, she remembered the sharp pain that had marked the end of her innocence. But even that pain was precious because it was the only gift she had to give to Lucien.

Though the shock when he had taken her…

He had stretched her beyond anything she could have imagined possible. But he had also reassured her, and it was Lucien's care and gentle treatment of her that would stay in her mind.

She had been full of lust, Tara remembered, smiling shyly down at him, but Lucien had turned it into more than that, and for that she would never forget him or this night of passion. Whatever life held for her in the future, this precious memory of Lucien Maxime, the Count of Ferranbeaux, would remain safely locked away in her heart.

Which would have to be enough for her, Tara told herself sensibly, settling down in bed a respectful distance away from Lucien. She might have fallen for a man called Lucien, but the man lying beside her was the mighty Count of Ferranbeaux, and she wasn't silly enough to imagine he felt the same.

CHAPTER THREE

Two years later.

STORM clouds, unusual for the time of year in the far south of Europe, threatened rain as Lucien Maxime, the Eleventh Count of Ferranbeaux, halted his Aston Martin outside one of his many grand country hotels. Opening the car door, Lucien unfolded his powerful frame, retrieved his pale summer-weight jacket and threw it on. Sensing he was being watched, he glanced up. An unremarkable plump young woman with an infant in her arms was looking down at him from a wrought iron balcony.

Tara Devenish.

The shock of seeing Tara again was like a battering ram to his solar plexus and time melted away as he stared back at her. Was it only two years since that night? He'd lost a brother and gained a niece in that time. Guy and Freya had been married little more than a year when they had been killed in a horrific car crash, and the baby in Tara's arms was their orphaned daughter.

The sight of his niece lifted his heart, but to see Tara holding Guy's innocent child sickened him. He could only think of that night when Tara had ground her hips so shamelessly against him. She'd been good—better than good, she'd been practised, she'd been excellent—and he had later learned his brother had thought so too.

With a sound of disgust he slammed the car door, remembering how, shortly before the fatal crash, Freya had publicly denounced Tara for sleeping with her husband. Who knew what Guy's state of mind had been when he'd embarked on that tragic car journey? The way he saw it, Guy's blood was on Tara's hands and if she thought that touching cameo of her holding Guy's child would soften him she was out of luck. Someone should have warned her he was not as gullible as Guy—he was a different man, a very different man. He couldn't believe he had misjudged her character so badly.

Uniformed doormen, in the claret and gold of the aristocratic Ferranbeaux family, raced to open the door for him, but he got there first. Swinging the door wide, he acknowledged each man in turn by name. He might loathe the fuss and deference many men in his position so avidly courted, but believed that was no reason to brush people off.

Today, with little time to spare, he moved swiftly on. He didn't need the heraldic shield emblazoned on each man's jacket to remind him why he was here. The honour of the family was once more under siege, another scandal pending; another situation for him to deal with before the rumours got out of hand. Guy's death had opened Pandora's box and now Pandora herself, or that young ingénue, as he had once so foolishly thought of Tara Devenish, was here at his command. She had been easy to manipulate, wanting to see where Poppy would live before agreeing to sign the adoption papers. He suspected she had seen this as one last chance to follow her sister's lead in securing a wealthy husband. Why else had it taken a single phone call to her lawyer from his for her to agree to this meeting?

His hand strayed to the cheque already made out to Tara in his breast pocket. It was an amount large enough to cover her expenses for Poppy to date, and to buy Tara out of their lives for good. Everything he did for his brother's child would be above reproach and on his terms. Uproot, unsettle and unmask was the way he had dealt with every scrounger who had plagued him since Guy's death and he saw no reason to change his modus operandi now. Tara Devenish might think she was very clever, in her sensible shoes and neat suit, wisely deciding to cut a very different figure to her wayward sister, but it would take more than a costume to convince him she was not the double-dealing slut Freya had declared her to be.

Tara could evoke surprisingly strong feelings in him, Lucien realised as thunder rumbled an ominous soundtrack to his thoughts. Two years ago he had thought her worth saving, and wanting to help out, he had left money for her on the night stand—lots of money, in the hope that she would use it to make a better life for herself. Now he felt he had been duped. He only had himself to blame. It wasn't even as if the signs had been unclear. Tara had been drenched in cheap scent and plastered in make-up, wearing an outfit designed to seduce. He could only conclude that his brain must have been lodged below his belt that night.

As the hotel manager hurried across the lobby to greet his Count, Lucien Maxime dealt swiftly with the formalities before making straight for the private sitting room where he had arranged for his meeting with Tara to take place. Lucien gave the room a quick once-over to check that everything was as he had requested. He had specified no flowers, no refreshments—no softening touches of any description. He would not allow Tara to imagine she had him in her sights again.

Having sent the manager to fetch her, he paced the room. Was it the prospect of seeing Tara or his niece that stirred such unaccustomed feelings in him? The truth, he accepted reluctantly, was that Tara had occupied far too great a part of his mind for the past two years. He had even considered looking for her to check on her progress, until of course the world's media had done that for him. The rage he'd felt then, when he'd read the newspaper reports documenting Tara Devenish's affair with his brother...

Even now it was all he could do to contain his anger. He shut that anger out, only to have another and even more disturbing image intrude on his thoughts—Tara, as she had looked in his bed.

He still wanted her.

That was the true torment.

As the minutes ticked by and there was still no sign of Tara, Lucien's expression darkened. She knew he was waiting for her to come down. At the very least, good manners demanded she should be on time for this appointment. Two years ago he had been prepared to indulge her, but no longer. Two minutes more and then he would go upstairs and bring her downstairs. An English court might have awarded Tara Devenish temporary custody of their niece, but both baby and Tara were under his jurisdiction now.

Seeing Lucien again was like a miracle—a miracle that made every part of her feel alive. She had forgotten

how beautiful he was and felt a shy embarrassment remembering how well they knew each other. When he
quit the car and the wind caught his hair, her body
reacted powerfully. When he straightened up all she
could think was how safe she had felt in his arms. But
when he looked at her and she saw the cold disappointment in his eyes her dreams collided with reality and she
rushed to shut that cruel look out.

She was too naïve for her own good, Tara reasoned,
walking across the room to put her sleeping niece down
to sleep. She could talk herself into believing anything:
that he had missed her; that he was coming to sweep her
up in his arms; that he was as eager to see her as she was
to see him…

That he had forgiven her never even came into her
thinking, because surely he must know the lies that had
been told about her couldn't be true…

Get real, Tara, she told herself impatiently. The
sordid facts were these: the first time she'd seen Lucien
in daylight was ten minutes ago. They'd met in a supper
club and had moved on to Lucien's hotel room, where
they'd had sex. At least, that was how he would see it.
She had woken to find him gone and in his place a wad
of money, along with the telephone number of a local
taxi company. Lucien had bought her services and, in
fairness to him, considering her lack of experience, he
had rewarded her well.

How red was her face now? Staring at herself in the
mirror, she patted her chipmunk cheeks, remembering
how, in her innocence, she had asked the man behind
the hotel reception desk on that night two years ago if
the Count of Ferranbeaux had left a forwarding address,
or perhaps a telephone number she could call. The man

had smirked as he'd told her that the Count of Ferranbeaux had checked out some time before, leaving no forwarding address, but that everything was paid for—including her, his expression had clearly stated.

She must have been the talk of the hotel, Tara thought, staring at the cruel reflection in front of her. The hotel staff must have laughed their heads off when she'd left. She only had to remember how pleasantly surprised and pleased with her Freya had been when she'd reported back to the bedsit. And no wonder— Freya must have known it was a long shot that Tara would interest Lucien.

Freya had been packing to leave with Guy, Tara remembered, and the fear and hollowness she had felt then came back to her now. Contemplating life without Freya had been dreadful. She had had no idea that one day their parting would be for good. Freya had smiled that morning and said gaily that it didn't matter if Tara never saw Lucien again, for there were plenty more where he came from, and that at least now Tara would know what to do with them…

Even today Tara shrank with shame as she relived that moment. She had been heartbroken, and had refused to believe that what Freya had said to her could possibly be true. Surely she would see Lucien again? Life would be unbearable if she didn't.

And now it was unbearable, because she must…

The only good thing to come out of all this was the lesson she'd learned; the life Freya had mapped out for her wasn't what she wanted at all.

Tara stared at her reflection in despair. She could breathe in, but she couldn't hold her breath for ever, and she couldn't drop three dress sizes in ten minutes.

Running her fingers through her mass of bright red-gold curls did little to tame her hair, but perhaps a little make-up would help…

If she had brought some with her.

She agonised, realising that high factor sun cream for infants and baby powder would hardly improve her looks. But it was all she had…

Grabbing the bottle of baby powder, she upturned it and sprinkling some on her palms, she wiped them across her burning cheeks…

Better…

Not much better…and certainly not perfect, but not so shiny, not so red…

Raking her bottom lip with her teeth, she wished it would plump out like it was supposed to do, and that she could reverse the colour of her lips and her cheeks—one so ashen and the other so red, but everything the wrong way round…

She tried hard to breathe steadily when she went to see Liz, the young nanny she'd brought with her. Liz had been trained by the same childcare college Tara had attended. Tara had paid her college fees with the blood money Lucien had left her; it had helped the shame somehow. Graduating with honours from that college had been the proudest moment of her life, and she must hang onto that now. 'Could you look after Poppy for me while I see the Count?' she asked Liz.

Tara had been offered a job on the staff of the college before tragedy struck, and when she had asked for leave to come and see where Poppy would be living the head of the college had been compassionate and had insisted she must bring Liz with her to Ferranbeaux. Everyone who knew Tara had read the newspaper articles condemning her and, without exception, her friends and colleagues had refused to believe a word they said. If only Lucien could be like them.

He wasn't, and there was no point wishing she could change him. Lucien had descended on the hotel like an avenging angel and was clearly not in the mood for negotiation, and now she had to meet him.

With every part of her trembling with apprehension. Lucien frightened her. His power frightened her. Anticipating the fact that he might look at her and laugh at her frightened her most of all.

She smoothed her skirt for the umpteenth time—her cheap skirt. But at least it fitted this time; she'd made sure of it. She checked her blouse—her cheap blouse. It was so cheap the fabric was like tissue paper, but if she kept her jacket fastened you couldn't see her bra…but then if she did that the buttons bulged…

Her breasts again…

Too big…

Everything about her was too big…

Including the big fat tears rolling down her cheeks. She hated them. They were a sign of weakness she couldn't afford with Poppy to defend.

Dashing them away, she sniffed loudly. Working out what was for the best, she decided on fastening the middle button on her jacket and leaving the other two undone…

Better.

Passable…

Not smart, but not bulging quite so badly now.

She was ready for whatever lay ahead.

Including Lucien Maxime, the Count of Ferranbeaux.

Lucien might be the all powerful Count of Ferranbeaux and hold all the cards, but did Lucien have the skills necessary to raise a child in the warmth and security of a loving family home? She wasn't going to let Poppy live in Ferranbeaux, cared for by strangers, just as she and Freya had been. Lucien could buy most things, but he couldn't buy time, and his business interests took up a lot of time…

Hearing a tap on the outer door of her suite, Tara whirled around. Her stomach was in knots. 'Come in…' Her voice sounded small, tremulous, pathetic, even to her.

'Ms Devenish?'

Tension seeped from her shoulders when the door opened and the hotel manager walked in. 'Yes?'

'Monsieur le Conte has arrived, and is waiting for you downstairs…'

Having powered through the gates in his twenty-first century equivalent of a fiery black stallion. Yes, she'd seen him.

'Ms Devenish?' the hotel manager prompted.

She was panic-stricken. There were too many holes in her plan. She needed more time. She had brought Poppy to Ferranbeaux because her lawyers had said she must, but whose orders were they obeying? Tara wondered now. She had seen Lucien's contempt for her as he must have seen her feelings for him. He believed the newspaper articles; ergo he believed her unfit to care for Poppy. He had come to take Poppy away. He thought her one more conniving woman who expected to profit from his brother's death.

As the hotel manager cleared his throat Tara swiftly refocused. Words had never come easily to her, and before the accident she had been content to remain in Freya's shadow, but with Poppy to protect that part of her life was over now. Tipping her chin, she spoke firmly. 'Thank you for delivering the Count's message. Please tell him I would like a little longer—'

'A little longer' would never be enough. It was better to get on with it, get it over with.

The manager's huff of surprise suggested he thought so too. But this was all just such a leap from the quiet life she had shared with Poppy since the accident. *All the more reason to hold their first meeting here, rather than in a public arena where she might make a fool of herself...* 'Could you ask the Count to come to my suite in say...ten minutes?'

'Here?'

The hotel manager seemed astounded, and Tara guessed that only years of training in the art of discretion allowed him to keep his opinions to himself.

Her relief was short-lived when he turned to go, for now the clock was counting down the seconds before she saw Lucien again—the man she adored, the man whom, the last time they'd met, had paid her off like a whore.

She listened intently to every sound, waiting for Lucien... She stilled her breathing, waiting for his footfall on the stairs. She wished she wasn't so tense. If she'd been more skilled in womanly wiles she might have known how to soften him, or if she'd been feisty, rather than hapless, helpless and useless, she might have known how to stand up to him. Unfortunately, she was none of these convenient things. She was barely twenty, and pretty clueless when it came to men. She was also plump, plain and poor and even her own sister had called her boring. Finding the right words was the least of her worries when she couldn't launch a good argument to save her life. And when it came to clothes and social graces...

By this point Tara's teeth were chattering with fear,

which was no help when her body was thrumming with awareness at the thought of Lucien just a few strides away. She knew he wouldn't have been idle while he'd been waiting. He would have been using this time to finesse his plan to eject her from Poppy's life.

She must blank her mind of fear if she was going to get through this. It was no good talking herself into meltdown; she must think things through clearly.

But, try as she might, the only thought Tara could come up with was that if Poppy had been old enough to pick a champion, her Aunty Tara should be last pick.

But who else was there to champion Poppy's cause? Lucien?

He'd make a far better job of it than she could, Tara reasoned, though he'd do it remotely through his servants.

Crossing to the window, she flung it open and inhaled deeply, hoping for a miracle. But there were no miracles—there was just Tara, an orphaned baby, and the Count of Ferranbeaux. That was the cast and it was up to her to decide whether she was content to play a role, or whether she would write the play. It was certainly time to get a grip. She wasn't the girl of two years ago; she was trained in childcare now and where Poppy's happiness was concerned she would fight tooth and nail to preserve it. It helped remembering a tutor at the college telling her she possessed a natural air of authority, and that it would raise her tiny stature in the eyes of a child. Would it work on the Count of Ferranbeaux? Somehow, she doubted it.

Lucien paced the room. Servants hovered, anxious to cater for his every whim. He waved them away. He wanted one thing, and one thing only, which was to have this meeting over with. Only then could he take his niece to a place of safety. At least, that was what he had been telling himself for the past half an hour, but the truth was more complicated. He wanted Poppy safe, that was a given, but Tara had dug her neat clean fingernails into some hidden part of him, and he was impatient to pluck them out.

He glanced at his watch again. How dared she keep him waiting? Didn't she think this meeting important enough to be on time? He had imagined she would be keen to get to work on him. Perhaps she was too busy luxuriating in the suite of rooms he had provided to remember her manners…

He stopped pacing to rake his hair. Even he was prepared to admit that last thought didn't reflect the Tara he knew. She might be cleaning the suite. He still remembered her surreptitiously picking up the napkin Freya had carelessly dropped on the floor, and then mopping up a pool of wine Freya had spilled on the table in the same graceful sweep. That Tara certainly didn't live up the sluttish image the media and her sister had painted.

He'd only just reassured himself with this thought when the old newspaper headline bounced into his head: The Unexpected Mistress. And the images of Tara in Guy's arms that conjured up made him physically sick. Lucien thought back to his own night with Tara; when she had thought he was sleeping she had whispered that there would be no other lovers.

So much for such adoration and innocence!

What was keeping the hotel manager? Lucien's eyes narrowed with suspicion as he stared through the open door towards the stairs. It was time to remember that Tara shared Freya's tainted blood. It was time to confront her.

CHAPTER FOUR

IT WASN'T just the aura of danger surrounding Lucien Maxime that drew attention as he crossed the hall. Tanned by the sun, and hardened by experience, Lucien married menace with style, which was a compelling combination. His tailoring was the best, and his only adornment a wrist-watch and a pair of gold cuff-links engraved discreetly with his crest. A man whose estates encompassed thousands of squares miles either side of the French and Spanish borders felt no need for the show other men considered necessary to boost their status.

Halting at the foot of the stairs, Lucien saw the hotel manager hurrying towards him. 'Where is she?' he demanded.

'Ms Devenish will not be coming downstairs, Monsieur le Conte—'

A spear of concern pierced him. 'My niece—'

'Is quite well, as far as I can determine, *monsieur*.'

Relief coursed through him, but his thoughts switched immediately to Tara. 'Then why does Ms Devenish choose to remain in her room?'

'Mademoiselle Devenish asked me to inform you that she will be happy to receive you in her suite in ten minutes.'

She will be happy? *She will be happy?*

Anger flared inside him. Not only had Tara defied his explicit instruction, she had dared to issue one of her own. It was time to call her bluff. How much could she have changed? Was she cowering in her suite? Or exulting in it at the thought that her pay cheque was only a few steps away? Whatever her motive, his niece would be raised in the security and stability of his family home and would not be left to the careless affections of some woman on the make. 'No matter,' he rapped in a tone that caused the unfortunate manager to press back against the wall. 'I will go to her.'

'Yes, Monsieur le Conte…'

As he mounted the stairs he fingered the cheque in the breast pocket of his jacket. If he had learned one thing from his father, it was that life had a universal currency. Tara would have her price. He would pay her off and then forget her. He stopped at the half landing and turned to see the manager still hovering and eager to be of service. 'I take it Ms Devenish is alone?'

'One other woman is with her in the suite with the child.'

'Who is this other woman?' His hand tightened on the banister at the thought of anyone standing between him and Tara. 'Do you know her?' It was not unheard of for men in his position to be trapped by unscrupulous women; witnesses could be hired and paid to make false accusations.

'I believe the other woman is the child's nanny.'

His lips pressed down as he thought about it. 'I was told Ms Devenish was acting as my niece's nanny. I was led to believe that was her profession now.' It had been reported to him that Tara had been awarded a diploma

48   COUNT MAXIME'S VIRGIN

in childcare, and he had imagined her running some sort
of agency from her front room.

When the manager remained silent he was forced to
draw his own conclusions. The 'nanny' was a useful
prop Tara had brought along to enable her to put aside
the child she said she cared so much about whenever it
suited her. *Just as her sister would have done...Freya
Devenish...* He formed the name silently with detesta-
tion as he continued on up the stairs. Freya Devenish,
with her wild blonde hair and her careless outlook on
life...Freya Devenish, a woman who had put her baby
second to her own pleasure. If Tara thought she could
trick him as Freya had tricked Guy— 'Don't announce
me,' he told the manager grimly. 'It is my intention to
catch Ms Devenish off guard.'

He would dismiss the nanny and find out Tara's true
intentions as well as what it would cost him to get rid
of her; no amount of money was too great to safeguard
his niece's happiness. The way he felt about Tara right
now, he couldn't wait to see the back of her, but was it
that thought driving him on, or some baser need?

The fact that she was in no hurry to see him stung him
far more than it should have done and urged him to brush
every remaining particle of compassion he might have
had for her aside. It didn't matter what he found inside
that suite of rooms—cunning schemer or last chance
saloon girl here in a bid to finish what she'd started two
years ago—either way, he was paying her off.

She had been listening so intently with every atom of her
being on full alert that when Lucien finally knocked on
the door a cry escaped her lips. Only a thin piece of wood
divided them. She knew it was him. She couldn't mistake

him when the sound of that imperative rap rang with his strength and his steely will, as well as his determination to have this over with. The hotel manager had made barely a sound, but then he had been schooled in the art of discretion, whereas the Count of Ferranbeaux saw no need for discretion, and why should he, when this was Lucien's suite, his hotel, his country—?

Where she was under his command...

Tara's body responded violently to the thought, though she tried to fight it. She tried warning herself that it was safer not to be in an advanced state of arousal when she opened the door, but her body wasn't listening. Her body was eager to feel Lucien's hand again, which left her a quivering mass of fear and apprehension.

And lust.

Her mouth dried. Other parts of her weren't quite so cooperative. How was she supposed to forget that night? She would never forget it, and neither would her body.

As the door shook with the force of a second knock, her teeth chattered as her mind sculpted the muscular frame behind the door. As the sound waves rippled through her head she could sense Lucien waiting outside like a predator preparing to pounce.

While she was what? The mouse with nowhere left to hide?

She exclaimed in fright as another knock sounded. 'Just one moment, please...' She sounded so strained, so timid and apprehensive and could only be thankful that she had remembered to slip the lock. Lucien was undiluted power, and she got the distinct impression that his shoulder would follow his fist if she didn't rush to answer the door.

Gulping in air, she smoothed her hair...checked her

skirt…her jacket…her collar… If the devil was in the detail, goodness knew what was in this short, plain, overweight package. If only she could close her eyes and open them to find herself tall and slim and elegant, with all the right words on the tip of her tongue.

'Tara,' Lucien bellowed. 'If you don't open the door, I'm coming in—'

'No, I'm here… Sorry.' She was actually standing rigid in the middle of the room with her fists clenched by her sides.

'Well, hurry up…Open the door.'

That beloved voice… He sounded so…utterly furious with her. She stumbled forward, disappointment and disillusionment propelling her. It only took one step…two to close the distance between herself and the door. 'I'll just open up,' she informed him unnecessarily, in an overly bright voice that sounded totally false.

'Well, come on, get on with it.'

She must stand strong. She stared at the handle, trying to concentrate. *She must stand strong.* Freya's tragic life and death was the most terrible warning. That was why she had got herself educated—made herself a better life—wasn't that worth fighting for?

Her mind blanked as Lucien rattled the handle again.

'What are you waiting for, Tara?'

She had to believe that somewhere beneath all the bitterness he was still Lucien, the man who had been kind to her.

She freed the lock with trembling fingers. Keeping her glance firmly fixed on the floor, she flung the door wide. She felt Lucien intimately in every part of her. He transformed her. He transformed her life… 'Monsieur le Conte…' Even now she felt more alive, but her voice was shaking. She had prepared for this moment so carefully, or thought she had, but nothing could have prepared her for the reality of Lucien Maxime, the Count of Ferranbeaux in person, only inches away.

Lucien strode into the room, walking straight past her without even acknowledging she was there. Halting, he turned and stared around the room.

He had ignored her.

And she? What had she done? She had stood there suffused with emotion, unable to speak. But the well of feeling inside her wouldn't be contained. 'Lucien, I was so sorry about your brother—'

His look froze the words on her lips. 'I'm not here to discuss Guy with you.'

His words rang in the silence, each one of them a death knell to her hopes. They carried a world of condemnation. Lucien had nothing but contempt for her and believed everything he had been told.

He shifted position and stared down at her from his lofty height. He couldn't have made it more apparent that this was now his room and she was an unwelcome visitor. Not only was it his room, this was his land, where Lucien's rule and Lucien's law prevailed.

And she was a lovesick girl who was already regretting the fact that on the one occasion when she had found some words to speak they were the wrong words.

But those words had come straight from her heart, Tara reasoned, and she had to believe Lucien was suffering for his loss as she was over Freya. She couldn't think him so cold-hearted he felt nothing.

And still she loved him.

She only wished she could reach out and offer him support—a thought so crazy she knew that only feelings so deeply ingrained and so precious to her could have prompted it. This man didn't want her. Lucien didn't want or need anyone's love. He was more polished and confident than ever.

Tara felt her spirit dwindling into nothing beneath Lucien's scornful gaze. She felt her fat cheeks burning beneath their pitiable coating of baby powder. Meekly, she turned to close the door behind him with exaggerated care. When she turned around Lucien studied her with a face that registered absolutely nothing. If his eyes showed anything at all, it was that she was an impediment to his day, and one that wouldn't hold his attention for very long.

'Tara…'

The deep, familiar voice held only irony and distaste. She searched his eyes, hoping for something softer in them, while Lucien searched for flaws, more things to count against her.

He'd find plenty, Tara concluded. She was still overweight, still plain, gauche and out of her depth in every way; she was still smoothing her skirt with repeated strokes of damp, shaky hands. 'Poppy's in the other room,' she managed, hoping to draw Lucien's attention away from her.

This failed too. He continued to stare at her while her cheeks continued to burn until she felt a faint sheen of perspiration starting to break out unattractively on her brow.

'I'll see my niece in a moment.'

This was her worst nightmare come true. This meeting was so awful, so completely at odds with her childish daydreams of seeing Lucien again, she felt strangely disembodied, as if this couldn't possibly be happening to her, because it was far too upsetting—far too final a rejection of her.

But it was happening. Lucien was here and he despised her. There wasn't a spark of humour in that deadly gaze. This was for real. You had better not be a whore, he seemed to be telling her, or I'm going straight to that nursery and taking Poppy from your care.

Tara realised she must have shivered at the thought because Lucien suddenly rapped, 'Why don't you ask the staff to close the windows if you're cold?'

Hysteria rose inside her and she almost laughed. If *she* was too cold? The roll of money Lucien had given her two years ago flashed in front of her eyes. That roll of money condemned her. He must be pleased to think she had never attempted to return it. He must imagine it would strengthen his case against her in court. Only she had the satisfaction of knowing she had used the money to pay her college fees. Perhaps it was that that allowed her to hold his gaze now. 'I know what you're thinking—'

'Do you really?' he said.

His voice was so deceptively mild, but his smile was cruel. Menace hung around him like a garland of thorns. Tara paused, unsure of herself but then the thought of Poppy gave her strength. All she could think of was the little girl sleeping down the corridor who depended on her. She would always stand between Poppy and the loneliness of being brought up by servants, whatever Lucien chose to throw at her.

'You were about to read my mind, I believe,' he prompted coldly.

Two years ago he had been kind. Two years ago he hadn't looked at her as if she was something he'd picked up on the sole of his shoe. Two years ago she had lost her heart, her virginity and, yes, ultimately her self-respect. And perhaps she should have stayed out of his way, but she hadn't. How could she leave Poppy's future for lawyers to fight over? She couldn't. She had to fight for Poppy. And so Lucien's path had crossed her own again. 'Do you believe everything you read in the newspapers?' she asked him quietly.

'Are you suggesting those reports were a pack of lies?'

'I had hoped you would know the answer to that—'

'So they were lies,' he said, cutting her off. 'Told by your own sister?'

Tara flinched at the look Lucien was giving her but, however much he provoked her, she would never speak badly of Freya. 'Freya was mistaken,' she said frankly.

'And you can prove that?'

Each time she spoke Lucien stamped on every word she said and kicked it aside. But she had always known this would happen, Tara reasoned, and only her wild imagination had allowed her to believe this meeting might be different. But she would defend herself—she had to. 'Whatever you think, I didn't sleep with Guy—'

'And I have the word of the "Unexpected Mistress" for that?'

Tara paled at Lucien's use of the cruel headline. 'Believe what you will of me, but I know the truth.'

Lucien remained unmoved and the ugly words he'd spoken hung between them like a challenge until she couldn't stand the tension any longer. 'Why would I want to sleep with Guy, when I'd slept with you?'

There was a flicker in his eyes, but his face remained a frozen mask she couldn't read. 'Why would I, Lucien?' She raised her voice. 'Guy talked to me sometimes... He asked me about Freya. He wasn't a bad man, Lucien... He was just—'

'Don't you dare presume to talk to me about my brother.'

He took a step forward, his eyes narrowed to slits of pure venom. His voice was pure ice, his stare heated. The anger between them was like a living force. She made herself hold that terrifying gaze, and was horrified to feel the energy slowly turning into something different.

No...

No... She shook her head, denying the evidence of her own eyes, her own body... This couldn't be happening... It mustn't happen...

She wasn't imagining it. In Lucien's eyes there was a look of pure appetite, a look she had not the slightest wish to ignore. It was the look of experience, of expertise, of understanding exactly what she needed. Her body responded powerfully to him. A look was enough to banish her fears and turn her dreams into a raging inferno of pure lust. Lucien knew this, and the understanding in his eyes only stoked the fires inside her.

And her heart? What about her heart?

A great black hole had swallowed up her heart, and all her foolish daydreams with it. Standing outside herself in these last few moments while rational thought was possible, she could see that for all his money and immense power Lucien was emotionally bankrupt, while she had too much feeling—enough to spare for him, if only he would accept it. But Lucien didn't want her compassion; Lucien wanted release. This wasn't an exercise to test her moral fibre, it was a simple basic need.

It had been so long and yet the touch of his hands on her arms made the lonely months melt away, and she was instantly transported back to a night two years ago, with the pleasure he'd brought her then fresh in her mind. She went with him in every way, every step of the way, holding his gaze and believing in something that didn't exist. It was no use trying to will her softer feelings into him because, whatever Lucien could or couldn't see, he was incapable of feeling.

He was careful with her, because she was so much weaker than he was, but they both knew where this was going. There was no point in dressing it up as something more when it was appetite pure and simple on both their parts. He had come here with the intention of taking the child home with him. Wanting Tara was an addendum, an inconvenience, an appetite he would sate and then move on.

'Do you want this?' His look silenced her.

Her lips parted and she closed her eyes. He stared hard at her. Her chest was heaving and she was flushed. 'Do you want this?' he repeated harshly.

She opened her eyes then and stared at him. 'I dreamed of this moment for two years,' she whispered.

Her lips...her full, trembling lips tempted him. Was this the slut he had read about, or could he believe her explanation about his brother? He leaned his weight against her and felt her body respond—did she respond only to him? He pulled back again and stared down at her. She met his gaze levelly.

Her eyes had grown dark and slumberous. Brushing her hair back from her brow as if he would find something to steal his trust away beneath its silky weight, he dipped his head and kissed her.

It felt like coming home.

He had to remind himself that he had many homes and didn't stay long in any of them.

He took off his jacket and tossed it on a chair before

helping Tara to remove hers. From there it was a scramble on Tara's part to lose the rest of her clothes. Last time, she couldn't wait to lose her knickers, he remembered. He lowered his zip and freed himself. Then sank into her and worked his hips to the accompaniment of Tara's frantic urging cries. She felt incredible and took him to places he hadn't been for two long years. Shutting his eyes, he closed out the doubt and concentrated on the pleasure streaming through him. He moved deeply and firmly, ramming her into the couch with each long, powerful stroke and, as the furniture shook and their makeshift bed inched its way across the room, some part of him registered that this was probably the most action the creaking floorboards had known in four centuries.

And still she wanted more.

'More?' he demanded, as if that didn't please him. 'More?' He worked his hips against her, upping the pace until she was shrieking with excitement.

'Yes!' she cried, unable to stop herself biting his shoulder like a wildcat as her fingertips raked his buttocks. 'Yes…!'

He finished her off, and was astounded by the strength of her climax. When she quietened there was no question of him soothing her down; he simply extracted himself with the least possible fuss and, standing up, arranged his clothes, before heading for the bathroom.

CHAPTER FIVE

Tara lay on the couch where Lucien had left her. Numb with disbelief that she could be so stupid. She had fallen at the first hurdle. She had betrayed Poppy. She had betrayed herself, proving herself to be no better than Lucien thought her. She was a weak and sorry excuse for a woman, and she despised herself thoroughly. It had taken her less than a moment to give way to carnal hunger. And to the pathetic longing to be loved and to be close to a man who could only think less of her. And what was she left with now? You couldn't wait for love, you had to earn it, and she had just thrown that chance away. She had thrown away her chance to be part of Poppy's life on a man who couldn't feel love, and all Lucien had proved was that he could get sex anywhere, any time, any place he wanted.

Realising the shower had been turned off, she quickly got to her feet and, hearing movement in the bathroom, she made a grab for her clothes. Lucien stormed into the room in a cloud of warm air and fresh soapy smells. 'Use the shower,' he said, towelling his hair.

His shirt was unbuttoned, his trousers unzipped...

She looked away. The moist and swollen place

between her legs was a humiliating reminder of the pleasure those strong, hard hips had dealt her. She still throbbed for him and, yes, if Lucien had wanted her now, she would have lain down for him again. Instead, muttering something unintelligible, she clutched her clothes as tight as a shield and hurried past him.

He rubbed his hair whilst absorbing everything around him, not least of which was a scent that took him back to boyhood and beyond. Baby powder. That was a bit different from the last time they'd met when Tara had been drenched in cheap perfume. He hadn't noticed the delicate scent before, but that was because he'd been consumed by rage, suspicion and contempt.

And now?

Now he was consumed by a different kind of rage. If Tara's intention had been to impress him with her newfound wholesomeness, she had just shot herself in the foot.

He finished fastening his clothes and, having folded the towel, stood by the window, waiting. He was impatient to see his niece and he hadn't met the nanny yet to approve her. He wouldn't scare the girl. He would wait for Tara to emerge from the shower and then she could introduce them. He was in no hurry. He felt quite relaxed now. Apart from the obvious, Tara had given him more than enough grounds to take the child to a place of safety…

But, regret—that was a different matter.

When Tara came back into the room he swung around, trying to fathom the attraction between them, for it was still there.

'Sit…'

She raised a brow, her gaze both wounded and de-

fensive. She had lovely eyes, he registered as she went
to sit on the edge of a sofa. She was more composed than
he might have expected. Who would think she had been
moaning in his arms only minutes before? He realised
then what it was she had gained in the past two years
that he hadn't been able to identify—it was presence and
dignity. He weighed these two attributes against Freya's
assertions regarding her sister. Tara could hardly be
mistaken for Guy's usual bedmate, either, which could
mean she was shrewder than her sister... Or it could
mean that what she was telling him was the truth.

Concentrating all his attention on the unexceptional
face, he attempted to rationalise his attraction to it. Apart
from a scattering of freckles across the bridge of her
nose, Tara's skin was as delicately tinted as the finest
porcelain and her smooth brow was framed by kiss curls
of bright gold hair. There was an appealing curve to her
mouth that suggested she tried to see the best in things.
She was quite a bit like Freya, but not nearly as pretty.
He might liken it to paint running on a portrait, making
the fine features a little less fine and the full lips a little
fuller. Tara's eyes were quite different from her sister's
too, and it wasn't just their striking colour; they lacked
Freya's flickering distraction and betrayed a depth of
thinking Freya had most assuredly lacked. That should
have been a warning not to trust Tara any more than he
would any other woman, but as he looked at her lips all
he could think was they promised more than deceitful
words, given the right circumstances. He knew he
wasn't ready to let her go yet.

'Can I offer you something to drink, Lucien?'

Lucien? Her boldness intrigued him. 'No, nothing,
thank you... We have another appointment in a few

minutes.' How long would that boldness last then? he wondered.

'We do?' She looked at him curiously. First confusion and then hope flared in her eyes. She thought he was taking her somewhere nice, perhaps.

He got up and moved away, turning his back on her. It was impossible to be this close to Tara without wanting more of her. His appetite, far from being sated, had merely been revived. He couldn't remember the last time a woman had affected him like this. Before he'd arrived at the hotel he had told himself that Tara Devenish was everything he despised. But seeing her again had fired a memory, and that was of a girl he'd known two years ago, a girl he had mistakenly believed to be an ingénue.

'I'll see my niece now.' He spoke brusquely in an attempt to shut out the past.

Tara rose from her seat without comment and led the way to the door. She put her finger across her lips when they reached the nursery, as if he needed reminding that his niece was sleeping. Perhaps it was this combination of the angelic and the sensual that intrigued him. Brushing that thought aside, he walked in as she held the door for him. He noticed her capable hands then. Tara's nails were blunt and clean. She wasn't frightened of hard work, he gathered, which explained why Freya had decided that Tara must take charge of Poppy while Freya tried her hardest to spend Guy's fortune. Freya's hands had been thin and had fluttered aimlessly, he remembered. They had always been carefully manicured, each bony finger tipped with blood-red acrylic.

'Isn't Poppy lovely?'

As Tara distracted him from these unpleasant

thoughts, he stared down at the sleeping baby. She was
right—his niece was lovely… Baby Poppy was sleeping
the sleep of the innocent, and he felt an overwhelming
urge to bring the infant under his protection. But, after
what had just happened between him and Tara, he
wasn't ready to discuss his brother's child with her, and
so he merely hummed agreement, refusing to be drawn.

As she had suspected, losing Guy had marked Lucien
deeply. Because he shunned feelings he was determined
not to show an Achilles heel to her, but she could feel his
pain. She could feel it as she could feel his love for Poppy.

'I'm ready to meet the nanny,' he said, pulling back.

That was her all over, wasn't it? Tara thought, as she
practically sprang to attention. She always waited to see
what would happen and then reacted to it. At some point
she must seize control of her life or be content to remain
in the shadows for good. For now she was the same
moth fatally attracted to a scorching flame, only now that
flame was Lucien instead of Freya. And it wasn't enough
to tell herself to be strong if she didn't have a plan…

So far no plan had occurred to her, Tara realised, as
she introduced a clearly awestruck Liz to the Count of
Ferranbeaux. Her sense of dread only increased when
Lucien leaned over the cot to adjust Poppy's blanket.
The look on his face told her all she needed to know.
Lucien had assumed control of Poppy's life, while she
was on the sidelines, shortly to be dismissed.

But wasn't Poppy more than worth fighting for?
Having identified the missing element in Lucien's make-
up, was she going to abandon her niece to such a cold,
hard man? It wasn't enough to hope and believe that everything would turn out right; she must make it so.

'I beg your pardon,' Lucien said politely as he brushed against her when he pulled back from the cot. He might have been speaking to a stranger.

'No problem,' Tara replied in the same bland tone. If she wanted to remain in contact with Poppy, she would have to fight. If she wanted to see Lucien again, she had to wise up.

He was standing by the door, indicating that she should leave the room before him. It was another example of Lucien asserting his authority, Tara realised, but she wouldn't fight him here in the nursery where they might disturb Poppy. She didn't have the resources to fight him anywhere, she reasoned as they left the room.

Closing the door silently behind them after leaving Liz in charge, Tara concluded that calm persuasion was the only weapon left to her. But would it be enough? Hadn't she seen the consequences of taking the line of least resistance? Sometimes you had to fight for what you believed in.

'You might want to brush your hair before we go downstairs.'

'My hair?' She patted it self-consciously. 'Why?'

'For the press conference…'

Tara's throat closed in terror. *A press conference?* She was hopeless in a crowd let alone in the spotlight.

'There have been enough scandals,' Lucien said calmly, as if meeting the press was an everyday event for him. 'Anything I do now must be seen by everyone to be scrupulous and above reproach, particularly in the run-up to adopting my brother's child—'

Tara's mind blanked. Lucien might have said something more, but she didn't hear it. She vaguely registered the fact that his lips were moving, but she couldn't hear, or think, or speak, or do anything other than stare stupidly at him as panic ran riot in her head. A press conference to announce the adoption? Since when? And what else would Lucien announce at this press conference? Her immediate return to the UK? He hadn't run anything past her, or even given her the courtesy of prior warning.

They'd been otherwise occupied, Tara remembered grimly.

'You knew about the adoption,' he pointed out.

'Of course I did... But you could have warned me about the press conference, Lucien.'

'I saw no need.'

No, he wouldn't. Lucien was used to this sort of thing; she wasn't.

'The child must have a father—'

'What did you say?' Tara's thoughts switched instantly from her own predicament to Poppy's future. And when her mind had computed Lucien's last few words she wanted to rail at him, *Poppy...Poppy* needs a father.

'It's for the best,' Lucien stated flatly.

For the best? There was a world of argument to counter that bold assumption, but as usual the smart words wouldn't come to her. And if they had, Lucien was already halfway out of the door.

'Wait, Lucien, please—'

As he opened the door and the noise of a crowd swept over her, Tara's courage failed. She had been pursued and pulverised by the media since Freya's death and the horror of it was still an open wound.

'Come along,' Lucien said impatiently, giving her no chance to refuse, unless she wanted to appear completely ineffectual in front of the world's press, that was.

Tara tried desperately to rake her hair into place before going downstairs, conscious that Lucien demanded the highest standards. She found an elastic band in her bag and, dragging her hair back, secured it, doubling up the wild curls and pulling them into a tight bun at the nape of her neck. Well, at least she looked a little bit respectable.

Polite as ever, Lucien waited for her, but she could see the brooding disapproval in his eyes and knew she hadn't got her hair nearly right. She also knew he wouldn't touch her, not even to smooth her hair. Sex was one thing, tenderness another, and that night of tenderness two years ago was all she was going to get from him. It was all she deserved. She was beginning to agree with him. No wonder Lucien had lost patience with her, when she was constantly proving herself to be such a clumsy, time-consuming handicap.

As they walked downstairs Tara could hardly believe the number of people who had crowded into the hotel, and all their faces quickly blurred into one hostile mask. No doubt basing their enthusiasm on past scandals involving the Maxime family, journalists had flocked into the town at Lucien's bidding. And no wonder, when between them Freya and Guy had probably sold more copy than any other celebrity couple on earth. Freya would have handled something like this with aplomb and even enjoyment, whereas she couldn't possibly...

'Lucien... Please... Wait...'

'For what, Tara?' he snapped impatiently, turning to face her.

'I'm sorry,' she said for the umpteenth time that day, self-consciously removing the hand she'd recklessly placed on his arm. 'It's just that I—'

'Not now, Tara,' he cut across her. 'And let me do the talking,' he instructed. 'All that's required of you is a pleasant smile and a nod of agreement from time to time. You can manage that, I take it?'

She remained mute. Lucien had dismissed her out of hand, and why wouldn't he when she had nothing of value to say? She followed him meekly down the stairs, trying to persuade herself that this was for the best and that Poppy would be far better off without her. She couldn't influence a decision, let alone the Count of Ferranbeaux. Why would any little girl want to be burdened with an aunt better known as an adulteress than as a childcare specialist?

As the swarm of faces in the lobby came into sharp focus it didn't help Tara's confidence that she was still throbbing from sex with Lucien. She was sure everyone must know every intimate detail of their relationship, and that just coming downstairs with the Count of Ferranbeaux had confirmed everyone's most salacious suspicion. They would think she was there as a convenience to be used. She should have thought things through before going along with whatever Lucien suggested. She should have thought about the consequences of having sex with him. She should have thought about the consequences of loving him, but it was far too late for that. She had no pride; there were no boundaries as far as Lucien was concerned and she had no strength to resist him. And, sure as the hell into which he'd plunged her, she had no common sense left.

They must have been halfway down the stairs when Lucien turned to deliver yet another instruction. 'However you feel about this situation, Tara, I'm asking you to keep your emotions in check. I ask this for Poppy's sake, as well as for the people who work for me on the Ferranbeaux estates—there have been enough scandals.'

As he broke off and passed a hand across his eyes, she told herself yet again that it was grief for his brother making him behave this way. Once again, her impulse was to reach out and comfort him, and she only just managed to stop herself in time.

'Are you listening, Tara? Do you understand what's at stake?'

As he spoke Lucien speared a look into her eyes, as if his harsh voice hadn't been enough to jolt her into the reality of their situation.

'Yes, of course I do.' She understood the Maxime family had become a source of ridicule, thanks to the notorious Devenish sisters, and she also understood that Lucien hadn't been given time to mourn his brother and that people needed time to grieve.

She tried to walk by his side, but Lucien quickened his step to get away from her. He radiated hostility, and as a path formed for them through the crowd of people in the lobby he continued to stride ahead of her. There were even people outside the hotel, standing on the steps, hoping to catch a glimpse of them, she noticed, and no wonder when Lucien was a grand Count from an ancient line and she was the wretch who didn't even know who her parents were. What a scandal! Tara guessed everyone must be saying. Lucien was such an imposing figure, which only made her more the mouse at his side—the dull little mouse with nothing to say.

She could feel herself growing hotter and more uncomfortable by the second, and knew she was attracting sideways looks. She could even hear some of the whispered comments. She was the Devenish sister who had slept with her sister's husband. She was the woman who had charge of Count's baby niece. How much longer before Lucien Maxime had charge of her? How long before he cast her off and forgot her?

In complete contrast to Tara's self-conscious scuttle across the crowded space, Lucien appeared completely at ease, even stopping to exchange the occasional pleasantry as he recognised one person or another. Tara marvelled at the way his pale linen suit barely seemed to have a crease in it, and the fact that his shirt looked as crisp as the moment it had left the shop. Lucien exuded class and money and confidence, and was every bit the elegant French count, with not one hair out of place to hint at the vigorous sexual activity he had been indulging in only a short time before. While she felt hot and wretched and completely out of sync as she hung back in the shadows, watching him talk with a body still singing from his touch, and the respectable outfit she'd put on earlier suddenly shrunk two sizes, or at least that was what it felt like.

As Lucien turned to glance at her, as if to check she was still there, she snapped to attention like a guardsman on parade. Perhaps he thought she'd run away and, goodness knew, she felt like it. Lucien had called this meeting to restore his family name, not hers, and she didn't doubt that he would. She knew the part she was expected to play. She was the ace up his sleeve, the disgraced sister who, having seen the light as shone by Lucien, had recognised the type of life the Count of Ferranbeaux could offer their niece and was prepared, not just to stand back, but to support him at this meeting and then conveniently disappear.

CHAPTER SIX

BUT even Lucien couldn't smooth all the snags away, Tara reasoned, as her wait continued. Yes, he could adopt Poppy, but what then? He'd have no alternative but to farm Poppy out for other people to look after. She must do something...say something...

At that moment the paparazzi swarmed and a barrage of flash bulbs exploded in her face. Her mind blanked and nothing but sheer black fright could get through. Holding her arms in front of her face, Tara tried to shield herself, and in doing so she almost tripped over the bottom step. She would have lost her balance completely had not someone caught hold of her, and it took her a moment to realise that the strong hand guiding her was Lucien's. He escorted her into the room that had been set aside for the press conference and asked her if she would like a glass of water before they began.

'Thank you...' No one could accuse Lucien of falling short on good manners. Who could say a wrong word about the Count of Ferranbeaux?

Lucien held a chair for her right next to his on the raised platform. She sat behind the long table dividing them from their audience, conscious that just being seated so close to him gave the impression that Lucien was controlling her. That was probably the right impression. The journalists were already filing in, while she waited apprehensively with her shoulders hunched and her head down, waiting submissively for whatever would happen next.

When Lucien rose to his feet the room went immediately quiet. He had no need of props or even a microphone to stamp his authority on their audience. With little more than a confident smile and a relaxed manner he put everyone at ease, and that command only increased when he responded fluently to questions in a number of different languages. She had *no chance* of standing against him, Tara thought as Lucien, having just wrapped up her final humiliation, turned to look at her for confirmation.

'Ms Devenish will, of course, be fully recompensed for her good care of my niece to date…and will use the money to start up a childcare agency…'

She found herself nodding agreement. She could see people thinking, how appropriate, how respectable, and knew that once again Lucien had saved the day. She was grateful, wasn't she? Of course she was. She nodded like an obedient child.

'And you, Ms Devenish?'

'I'm sorry…?' Tara's face flamed red as the attention of the room was drawn to her. Everyone was staring at her. She had been so lost in her thoughts that it took her a moment to rattle her brain cells into some sort of order and realise that someone other than Lucien was speaking to her. 'I… I'm not sure I heard your question…'

A number of disapproving sounds and knowing looks were exchanged before a quietly spoken man from a national television company repeated the question for her, but before she had chance to answer him another reporter chipped in with, 'Surely you must have some opinion on your sister's little girl coming to live so far away from you. Don't you worry that you'll never see her again?'

'Of course I do—' Icy fear twisted a knot in her stomach as Lucien stared down at her. What was it he had said she must do?

Inclining his head in a gesture only she would see, he flashed another heat-free smile, no doubt meant to encourage her to remember his instruction.

Nod your head and smile pleasantly—that was it!

She lifted her chin as a puppet might when the strings were drawn tight. The next move of her head must be downwards, and the nod must be accompanied by a re-assuring smile and a relaxed air, as she stared like everyone else in awe and admiration at the man who would take care of everything…

'Ms Devenish… Ms Devenish…'

Tara's hesitation had provoked the reporters into baying her name with increased urgency and, seeing Lucien was on the point of silencing the uproar, she knew this was her one and only chance to speak up. Unless she liked the look of the back seat in Poppy's life, that was.

Rising clumsily to her feet, she stood, face on fire, wishing she'd thought to loosen the waistband on her skirt. It was so hot in the room, and while everyone cla-moured for her attention she felt as if she were slowly expanding and becoming more a figure of fun than ever. Some of the hardened hacks were laughing openly at her, whispering together with their hands covering their mouths, and their eyes were so cruel. And the women were so thin. Why was that? How could she stand against them? A massed *them* against solo *her*. Not even Lucien was on her side; she had no one.

She couldn't stand against them. Where would she begin?

By waiting for silence, Tara's inner voice counselled.

It took much longer for silence to fall for her than it had for Lucien, and throughout every moment of that time Tara knew she was being laughed at. But there came a point when she realised it couldn't get any worse and so she held her ground. She also held the table, so tightly her knuckles showed white beneath her skin.

At least she'd had plenty of time to list the things she'd never done by the time the room finally went quiet, along with the things she never would do unless she spoke up now. She had put herself through college and had been awarded a scholarship to continue her education. She had been offered a place on the staff. If she could do that, surely she could handle a press conference? If she wanted to remain part of Poppy's life she had to, and if she wanted to see Lucien again, she must.

'Thank you, ladies and gentlemen…'

Perhaps it was her clear voice that shocked everyone into silence. Consciously relaxing her hands, she let go of the table. It took her a moment, but she got there. Sucking in her stomach at the same time as her breath, she continued, 'I'm sure you all appreciate what a difficult time this has been for both of us—' She glanced at Lucien then, but was careful not to let her glance linger. Having fought so hard for composure, she wasn't about to squander that composure on the altar of the Count of Ferranbeaux's smouldering mystique. 'But, hard though it is for us to speak so soon after losing people we loved, I know I speak for both the Count and myself when I say we have only Poppy's best interests at heart—' In her peripheral vision she was surprised to see Lucien nodding agreement.

'Absolutely,' he murmured.

She made the mistake of looking at him again, which prompted a minute nod, as if he wanted her to know he was pleased with her for toeing the party line: his party line.

'Pretty words,' one of the reporters interrupted. 'But what does this actually mean, Ms Devenish?'

The woman's voice was so cold that Tara's heart began to race again. She knew this was the defining moment when she must speak up or sit down. 'Nothing has been decided yet, but until a formal adoption order is made by the court…' she steeled herself for what she was going to say next '…I shall be travelling with the Count and our niece to the Count's family home in Ferranbeaux—'

The room exploded into uproar. It seemed like forever before the press pack quietened again, and when they did Tara was surprised to find that she felt much calmer, as if for once in her life she had hit on exactly the right thing to say. 'I will be staying in Ferranbeaux until it is decided how to ensure the best outcome for our niece,' she repeated with more confidence.

As she sat down cries of 'Why?' and, 'Is this right, Count?' nearly deafened her.

As Lucien stood to answer the questions, Tara was sure she wasn't the only one who felt the immense power he exuded, and the immediate silence proved this.

'Is this right?' he repeated mildly, directing his words at the acid-tongued woman. 'That was your question, wasn't it?'

Tara felt the anticipation in the room increase, provoked by the Count of Ferranbeaux's magnificent, yet brooding presence. 'I think Ms Devenish is quite capable of speaking for herself,' he said with a casual gesture.

Had Lucien really said that? Tara stared at him, unsure of the evidence of her own ears. She didn't know what to make of it. Was he endorsing her stand? Was Lucien supporting her? He certainly wasn't making a fuss about her visiting his home, which was so much more than she had hoped for.

Her body responded predictably to this new development, thrilling to the news, while doubt lost no time attacking her. The harsh words would come later, she reasoned. She had disobeyed Lucien's clear instruction to keep her thoughts to herself. As he leaned across to say something to her, she started in alarm, expecting the worst.

'They're waiting for you to speak,' he murmured. 'Surely you haven't finished yet?'

Was that a hint of humour in his gaze? She stared up at him, transfixed.

'Perhaps you'd like me to speak for you?' he suggested dryly.

This time there was doubt in her mind that Lucien was not only surprised by her stand, but rather approving of it. Her heart thundered in double time when she registered another flicker of amusement. If it hadn't been combined with such a hard set of his mouth she might even think the Lucien of two years ago had returned to her.

She couldn't hope for that, Tara decided sensibly. She had to stand on her own two feet. Determinedly, she did just that. She felt better this time—stronger. It was up to her to decide what she took from this room.

'I expect you all think this is an unusual arrangement…' Singling out the most influential reporters, she directed her comments to them. 'But I'm equally sure you can all understand that I have to be certain that Poppy will be happy here in Ferranbeaux. I've been caring for my baby niece since my sister's tragic death…' She paused for a moment to collect herself, aware that this was no time for a show of emotion. 'I'm very close to Poppy,' she admitted quietly, 'and the Count of Ferranbeaux understands that…' This time she did look at Lucien and, holding his gaze, she missed the murmur of approval in the audience.

'And how do you intend to do that?' the woman who had clearly cast herself in the role of Tara's nemesis demanded.

'By making sure that this—Poppy's first visit to her uncle's home—is made with those Poppy knows and trusts around her.'

'Are you accusing the Count of neglecting his niece?' the same woman called out.

Tara refused to be provoked. 'No, of course I'm not saying that.' How many lies had been told and believed about her? Would she condemn Lucien to the same fate? 'The Count has worldwide responsibilities and many calls on his time, and our niece is very young. For those reasons alone, he has not been able to see as much of Poppy as he would have liked—'

'Is that true, Count?' the woman called out.

Lucien smiled faintly. 'Ms Devenish seems to have everything covered—'

'Ms Devenish?' the same woman barked, 'do you have anything else you'd like to say?'

'No, I think that's it—'

'You wouldn't care to elaborate on your visit with the Count?' the woman pressed in a way that hinted at something seedy.

Tara kept a pleasant look on her face. She had no intention of losing her temper or inadvertently supplying some juicy detail that could be used to underpin the flagging sales of some red-top scandal-rag. 'There's nothing more for me to say, other than the Count will be seeing a lot more of his niece in the future—'

This time even Tara couldn't silence the storm of questions and one voice, predictably, rose above the rest. 'Is this right, Count? Your press office led us to believe that you would be taking over *full* responsibility for your niece and that Ms Devenish would be returning to England without the little girl, but with a rather sizeable cheque?'

This time even the most hardened reporters fell silent. They all knew that what had been said was a terrible slur on Tara's character. Tara tensed as she waited to see how Lucien would handle it.

He levelled a long, considering stare at her.

She must hold his gaze. *She must.* Lucien's expression held fire and ice, but which of those was for her? He could hardly have been expecting her to invite herself to his home, after all.

The menace in the air increased as he stood up and she could have heard a pin drop as he began to speak. 'Ms Devenish has explained the current situation as well as anyone can, and I confirm that the arrangements are exactly as she has stated. If a different version of events is reported *anywhere* it will be rigorously fought by my legal team in court.'

This time the silence had a different quality; no one

wanted to risk their job by exposing the company they worked for to the expense of defending a high profile libel case.

Tara was stunned by the fact that Lucien had chosen to defend her and that he had issued a threat that no one in the room could afford to take lightly. He had fought fire with fire and had done so with his customary compelling charm, but she was willing to bet no one had missed the underlying threat in his words.

'If that's all…?' He barely paused to take breath before adding, 'I'm bringing this meeting to a close. Are you ready?' he added, turning to her.

He had never seemed more magnificent to her, and all the people she had been so scared of paled into insignificance in the face of Lucien's reassuring presence.

'I'm ready,' Tara confirmed, standing up.

She walked out of the room at his side, but when the door closed behind them she became aware of the tension he'd hidden so well. Lucien had put on a good act for the press, but she had thrown him a curving ball. He might be escorting her through the crowded lobby as if she were minor royalty, with one arm outstretched in front of her face and his hand in the small of her back, but his grim expression wasn't solely directed at the most persistent of the hacks following them. Lucien hadn't expected the girl in the shadows to take a step forward and make a statement, and was only now taking on board the fact that where Poppy was concerned Tara had a mother's instinct and a woman's guile, and when it came to making sure her niece's childhood was very different from her own there were no dragons fierce enough to frighten her away.

'Wait there for me, will you?' he said distractedly as

a reporter for one of the major television companies waylaid him.

Tara stared at the chair Lucien was indicating. It was stuck away in a corner out of the way and she didn't want to go back to the shadows. The bare truth was, she wanted Poppy *and* Lucien, but Lucien wasn't some prince in a fairy tale on a quest for a winsome bride; he was one of life's leaders, and if he was searching for anyone it was a soul mate, not some compliant drip content to sit where she was told. If she wanted Lucien, she had to fight, and she didn't have any God-given right to care for Poppy, she had to fight for that too. But if she had to prove she had a backbone then Lucien must prove he had a heart; Poppy deserved nothing less. Fate had offered them both a chance to mend the past and provide Poppy with a happy future, and she had no intention of throwing away her side of the bargain through self-doubt.

Which was easier said than done when you looked like a dumpling tied up with string, Tara reflected dryly, having caught sight of her reflection in one of the many gilded mirrors. What she saw was all grey and putty-coloured and overweight, with red-gold hair bundled back as if to try and prove how respectable she was. She looked a mess. It was time to smarten herself up and not be content with what she thought people expected her to be.

Be herself? The shadows seemed tempting suddenly. Who was she really? It was early days in the rapidly changing world of Tara Devenish. Hanging onto who she wanted to be was proving harder than she had imagined. But she could work at it. Losing Freya had drained her emotional bank and she was only just beginning to understand how depleted that had left her. If she fell back to pathetic status, it was understandable, but it wasn't something she could afford to do. She had to stay on red alert and recognise those wimpish tendencies and kick herself out of them, if she had to.

While Lucien was still talking she took the opportunity to return to the nursery. She stood outside the door of her suite for a moment composing herself. No way was she taking the remnants of her self-doubt inside. There would be no scenes in the nursery, and no alarm caused to Liz or Poppy. Whatever she felt inside, whatever doubts assailed her, she'd keep them to herself.

Taking a deep breath, Tara opened the door and was instantly filled with happiness and relief to find Poppy gurgling happily in her cot. Wasn't this all that really mattered? Poppy's happiness was everything to her. She might have her setbacks, but she would never allow them to impinge on Poppy's life.

Having explained what had happened downstairs to Liz, Tara started to help her to pack up their things. 'Do you have any make-up?' she asked when they were almost finished.

'Make-up?' Liz looked at her.

Tara put down the sensible knickers she'd been folding, realising that her request must seem odd, but she had the idea that if she faced the world with a more confident-looking face she would be treated differently, even by Lucien. Anyway, she was going to give it a try. 'I've forgotten mine,' she explained.

Since when did Tara use make-up? Liz's surprised look seemed to say.

'Mascara, blusher, lip gloss?' Tara suggested hopefully. Well, it had to be an improvement on baby powder.

'Hypo-allergenic, for sensitive skin?'

'Perfect,' Tara confirmed. It was time to experiment. She might make a mess of it, but what harm could it do? She could always wash her face.

CHAPTER SEVEN

TARA'S courage under fire during the press conference had impressed him but why had she disappeared, and was it impatience or desire surging through him as he mounted the stairs to find her? He had been on the edge of his seat throughout the meeting, ready to spring to his feet and bail her out the moment it proved necessary. It hadn't. She might have been at a disadvantage and vulnerable on any number of fronts, but she had handled everything with cool aplomb. Just when he had cast himself in the role of white knight, she hadn't needed him. That had thrown him, but now he was prepared to consider that he might have made an arrogant miscalculation where Tara was concerned. The least he could do was to congratulate her on a job well done. She had shocked him, that was for sure, but by the time he turned onto the corridor leading to her suite he had calculated that she must be out of surprises.

Wrong.

She opened the door at his first knock and said calmly, 'Come in, Lucien.'

The surprises didn't end there. She had let her hair down in more ways than one. 'Tara...' His expression must have given him away but, as always, she kept her cool.

'Would you like to sit down?' she said, affecting not to notice his double take. 'We're almost finished here…'

She went to turn away, but something in his gaze must have held her. 'Yes?' she said, displaying the composure he'd seen downstairs, but this time with a slight edge of apprehension clouding it.

'You look different,' he said. That was a major understatement. She had freed her hair so it bounced round her shoulders like a wayward cloud of red-gold curls, and had put on some make-up. Not too much, and not expertly applied either, but enough to frame her turquoise eyes in a smudge of black, and to outline her lips with some gloss that caught the light.

'Different good?'

Now he understood her apprehension. 'Good,' he said, nodding with approval. He saw her relax and thought how pretty she looked, or maybe he'd never looked at her properly before, he decided.

She relaxed enough to give him a rueful half-smile. 'Welcome to the land of milk and vomit and no sleep, Lucien—'

He laughed and then stopped abruptly, wondering what the hell he was doing.

As Liz bustled past with an armful of baby clothes, he stood aside. In every other way he was swept up into the hustle of packing up and shipping out. 'Can I help you with that?' he asked as Tara hefted a box full of baby equipment onto the table.

'You could carry it downstairs for me—unless you'd like to call a member of your staff…?'

The changes in her weren't so subtle. 'Give it to

me,' he said, thinking the press conference had done her good.

'Well, thank you…' Her smile was warm as she held his gaze. 'And thank you for defending me downstairs—'

'Seems to me you did a pretty good job of that all by yourself…'

'But it was nice to have you back me up.'

'I can't stand bullies,' he told her frankly, 'and that woman was bullying you.'

They looked at each other for a moment and then her gaze slipped away. He knew what she was thinking, because he was feeling it too, down deep in his groin.

'Don't thank me,' he insisted, conscious of the growing pressure. 'I won't stand by and do nothing if someone takes you on—'

'Someone other than you, you mean?' she suggested quietly.

Something was happening between them—her growing confidence, perhaps, shifting things up a gear. Whatever, he liked it. Tara's quiet strength sparked enough electricity between them to light a small town. But he didn't allow himself the luxury of feelings and could switch off as fast as she could switch on the light. He changed tack to the subject they should both focus on. 'At least you should be reassured now,' he said confidently and, when she looked at him, he added, 'You've carried the responsibility of Guy's child single-handed up to now, and I thank you for that—'

'Poppy was my sister's child too,' she said interrupting him.

'Of course,' he said, determined to find the path of

reason through all of this. 'But you can only agree that Poppy will have a happy and settled life with me—'

'Can I, Lucien?'

'I don't know what more you can ask.'

'A woman's touch would be nice.'

He hadn't expected her to question him, but he was learning that the surprise attack was Tara's strength. She had been so quiet and retiring up to the moment she'd made her statement in the press conference, he still expected her to fall in line. He would have to re-jig his thinking where Tara was concerned, quite considerably, starting now. He didn't trade in false expectations, and sometimes you had to be cruel to be kind. 'Until I take a wife, our niece will have the best nannies that money can buy.'

Her gaze flickered, but she stated calmly, 'Money can't buy love, Lucien.'

He hardened his heart. 'Clichés, Tara?'

A wounded shrug rippled across her shoulders.

'Love comes at a price in my experience—'

'Then I'm sorry for you, Lucien.'

'Save your pity.' He didn't like the way she made him feel.

The mood changed, darkened.

'Finish packing and then I'll carry those things down for you.' He turned his back on her and went to stand in front of the open window. The storm had rolled back to reveal a watery sky streaked with cirrus cloud. He was still with the storm clouds, tense and brooding. Bottom line: Guy was dead and nothing would change that, but he could do something about Tara Devenish. 'I'd like to leave as soon as we can,' he said without turning round.

He heard her leave the room and immediately felt

the lack of her. She had the knack of unlocking parts of him he'd rather not inspect too closely; he didn't thank her for it.

'We're ready,' Tara announced some time later. He turned to see her carrying Poppy in her arms. He quickly stifled any response the tender tableau provoked.

'Good,' he said briefly. 'I'll call for the limousine—'

'How will you get back, Lucien?'

'With you…' He could tell she hadn't expected that.

'What about your car?'

'Someone will collect it.' He guessed she had been hoping for some time alone with Poppy. He sensed her uncertainty about the future, but when she saw him assessing her she tipped her chin and firmed her jaw.

'Fine,' she said mildly.

He had to wonder then, why was he taking her to his stronghold? Ferranbeaux was more than a medieval city of national importance to him—it was his home. Did he really want to introduce Tara to his home, to his staff and to his people? If she really was this decent, caring individual, why had she betrayed her sister so spectacularly? Freya had hardly been perfect, but why would she have wrecked her own sister's chance of a decent life by dragging Tara's name through the mud? Was the truth exactly as the newspapers had stated? Had Tara found Guy, or rather Guy's substantial bank account, irresistible? As his suspicions mounted, he asked himself if he had just been smooth-talked into a corner for the first time in his life. 'I'll see you downstairs,' he told her brusquely.

Tara saw Poppy and Liz settled comfortably in the back of the spacious limousine before taking her seat. She was both excited and apprehensive at the thought of visiting Lucien's home. It was one thing standing up for Poppy in a press conference and vowing to change her personality, and quite another entering the lion's den. She had tried to imagine what Lucien's home might be like and just couldn't; there were so many layers to him, so much he kept hidden. Plus, she didn't have that many visits to medieval castles for her imagination to draw on. In fact, this one would be the first. If she pictured anything, it was towering grey stone walls and a forbidding interior with lots of animal heads staring down sadly from the walls. The only thing that mattered, Tara reminded herself as they waited for Lucien to join them, was to satisfy herself that the arrangements he'd made for Poppy were the right ones. It really didn't matter what she thought of Lucien's home, her only concern must be—was it the right place for a little girl to grow up?

Her only concern?

Tara's throat dried as Lucien came into view. She must be mad if she thought that. She breathed a sigh of relief when he headed for the front seat next to the driver, where the chauffeur was holding the door for him. A special car seat had been fitted for Poppy, and she was slumbering in the row behind Tara, with Liz sitting next to her. Not wanting to disturb them, Tara had chosen a row to herself in the stretch limo. It was a good choice, she congratulated herself now. In spite of the effort she'd made to spruce herself up, she felt exhausted and fat. She was into small pleasures at the moment, she realised ruefully as she lowered the zip on her skirt with a sigh of relief. Hitching it up, she sighed with the first real pleasure she'd felt that day.

She had barely had a chance to relax when the door

swung open and Lucien took the seat next to her. 'What are you doing here?' He'd shocked her into defensive mode.

'In my own car, do you mean?' He glanced pointedly at her thighs before leaning forward to tap on the glass, the signal for the driver to pull away.

What a perfect end to a perfect day, Tara reflected. Lucien was his customary elegant self, while she had her skirt hitched up ungracefully!

'I'm sorry to have kept you waiting—' he glanced at her thighs again '—but I see you've made yourself comfortable.'

'That's right, I have,' she agreed, struggling inelegantly to right her clothes.

'Can I help you?'

'No, thank you, I can manage… What are you doing?' she exclaimed as he leaned over her.

'Fastening your seat belt.'

As Lucien turned to look at her, their faces were dangerously close. She held her breath. And let it out in a ragged sigh when he pulled away.

The hairpin bends on the steep mountain road made it hard to spot the walled city of Ferranbeaux until they were almost on top of it. But as Tara stared through the tinted windows of the limousine into the gathering darkness she finally saw something rising out of the mist. 'Is that a castle?' She was excited in spite of her determination to remain calm. Calm was one thing, but when calm was challenged by a fairy tale kingdom… She could see slim shadowy towers topped with inverted ice cream cone shaped roofs. The terracotta pantiles coating them glowed faintly red beneath a purple sky.

It was like Cinderella's castle…though, just as she had feared, the fairy tale castle was completely enclosed by towering stone walls.

'That's my home,' Lucien explained. 'Do you like it?'

Did she like it? A walled city that took up a vast acreage on the summit of a sprawling hill with a castle set like a rough hewn jewel at its centre? She most certainly did like it, though, like Lucien, it held more secrets than she knew, Tara suspected. 'So this is your place in the hills,' she murmured.

'One doesn't like to boast,' Lucien said, responding to her subtle irony.

'Doesn't one?' She couldn't resist a small smile. 'Do you actually live in the castle?' she said, turning to him.

'I do.'

The look in Lucien's dark, mesmerising eyes shot heat through her. 'That must be nice,' she said, trying hard to concentrate on something other than his mouth.

'Very nice,' he agreed in a way that suggested he could read her mind.

And now she couldn't stop her gaze wandering back to him. He was looking out of the window, fortunately. Lucien and Ferranbeaux had the same mixture of magic and menace about them and couldn't have been better suited.

The limousine was forced to slow as it approached a wooden bridge that crossed an illuminated dry moat. As they rumbled beneath a towering stone archway the car was plunged briefly into darkness, and Tara thought it was like moving back in time. Certainly, with every yard she travelled she was moving deeper into Lucien's territory.

And ever more under his control? She shivered inwardly. Whatever resolutions she might have made, she was only twenty, with little or no experience of life and men, while Lucien was the mighty Count of Ferranbeaux, an older man who wielded immense power and had almost limitless wealth at his disposal—hardly a fair contest!

Added to which, her rebellious body never missed an opportunity to respond to her erotically charged thoughts. Lucien was a hard, sensual man who had awoken appetites in her she had barely guessed at. Realistically, how long could she resist him? She didn't need the buzz of sitting this close to him to remind her how enthusiastically she had succumbed to his dark arts in the past, and just revisiting these forbidden thoughts was enough to make her wonder if she was destined to live the life Freya had mapped out for her after all.

She stole a glance at Lucien's proud face in profile. Like the fortified city he called home, Lucien was a timeless force of nature, and one she craved. He blended seamlessly into the wild and rugged terrain over which he ruled, and she wanted his attention, though she realised she had no hope of touching his heart. She had no intention of being anyone's mistress either, Tara determined, firming her jaw. She had to find a way through this somehow... As she stared blindly through the window, something caught her attention and it was a distraction she welcomed. There were flags and bunting everywhere, suggesting Ferranbeaux could be a happy place too. 'Has there been a celebration?'

'Of course,' Lucien confirmed. 'The people of Ferranbeaux are welcoming Poppy home.'

Of course. Tara's heart sank. She knew that, but it didn't stop her worrying at the thought she would soon be separated from Poppy, and possibly for good.

Lucien's home might look like a fairy tale castle on a hill, complete with twinkling lights and mullioned windows, but it wasn't her home, Tara reminded herself sensibly as the limousine slowed to negotiate golden gates leading into a vast cobbled courtyard. Still, it was hard not to be just a little starry-eyed when the vehicle halted at the foot of a wide expanse of sweeping stone steps. It was impossible not to let her imagination have full rein and picture elegant partygoers alighting from their carriages…the ladies in silks and satins in all the colours of the rainbow, escorted by tall, elegant men…

'Tara?' Lucien murmured, pointing out the fact that his chauffeur was holding the door for her.

Covering for her distraction, she tried to climb out with a modicum of grace. Well, that was a pipedream, but fortunately Lucien's reflexes were as fast as his brain, and his arm shot out to save her. 'This is very grand,' Tara said awkwardly, regaining her balance to stare up at the imposing façade of the first castle she had ever visited. She didn't belong here, though Lucien, with his small party of two awestruck women and a babe in arms, was understandably relaxed—this was his home after all.

He shrugged after steadying her on her feet. 'So what do you think of Poppy's new home?'

Tara tensed and instinct brought her closer to Poppy. 'I'll take her now,' she told Liz. Tara felt as if her stomach had been stitched with a running thread and someone had pulled it tight. She didn't need Lucien reminding her that her time with Poppy was limited and each precious moment was running through her fingers like sand through an hourglass.

She slowly turned full circle after Liz handed Poppy

over to her, trying to take everything in. She guessed that unless you'd been brought up in circumstances like this you would never get used to the sheer scale of the place Lucien so casually called home. She couldn't even see the boundaries of the courtyard, and the forbidding walls were decorated with crenellated battlements where, centuries before, archers must have patrolled. It was quite a bit different from the orphanage where she and Freya had grown up...

'Shall we go inside?'

Tara was still staring in wonder at a stone fountain where glittering plumes of water spewed from the mouths of fiery steeds mounted by fierce-looking stone warriors when Lucien dipped his head to speak to her and it took her a moment to refocus. 'Did they model those statues on anyone in particular?' she wondered, speaking her thoughts out loud.

'I'm not that old,' Lucien informed her dryly.

Apprehension and heat rippled through her as Lucien held her gaze. She was so acutely tuned to him she couldn't pretend not to interpret that look.

'Well, are you going to come inside?'

Tara stared up at the double doors of the castle. The ancient oak looked thick enough to withstand a siege, and each door was studded with iron bolts. Those doors were sturdy enough to keep an army out, Tara concluded—or anyone they chose to in. She was shivering with apprehension even as she nodded and followed Lucien. For now she had nowhere else to go.

Embracing Poppy protectively, Tara dropped a kiss on her baby niece's smooth brow. She had to make herself believe that a court of law would not compare her modest rented home back in England unfavourably to this. She had to believe in miracles, in fact. She was very proud of the tiny nest she'd made, but her concern that it would be considered an unsuitable destination for the aristocratic niece of the Count of Ferranbeaux seemed entirely justified now.

'Can you manage to carry Poppy up the steps?' Lucien asked her.

'Of course I can.' She knew she sounded defensive, and she was, but she had to be careful not to communicate her fears to Poppy. 'This is your new home,' she whispered, gazing up the steps. 'Isn't it lovely?' And the castle was lovely. The ancient stone gleamed silver in the moonlight, and after the storm the air was cool and fresh. The ground had received such a good drenching she could smell the fragrant minerals in the earth and, however hard she tried to fight off the charms of Lucien's stern grey home, just as she found him mesmerising, Tara was fast discovering that the castle of Ferranbeaux had wasted little time in wrapping its magic around her heart.

But as she wouldn't be given a chance to grow attached to it, Tara reflected sensibly as she started up the steps, she should concentrate her mind on whether it was a suitable home for Poppy. She was just getting a hold on this common sense approach when Lucien took hold of her arm. She knew he was just making sure she didn't stumble, but electricity shot through her at his touch. She flashed him a smile of thanks, but as the double doors swung open in front of them and she saw the line of uniformed staff waiting to greet them Tara realised her ordeal had only just begun.

CHAPTER EIGHT

SHE must concentrate on the fact that Lucien's castle was a much better environment for Poppy than the flashy penthouse Guy had bought for Freya, Tara decided as her courage deserted her in floods. Every face of every member of staff was turned her way, and it took her a moment to register the fact that people were smiling at her as well as at the baby in her arms. The castle might be huge but, with the addition of some warm-coloured tapestries and a giant-sized rug in the marble entrance hall, could give the illusion of cosiness. Despite its size, her initial impression was that this could be a proper home, with a proper garden, even if that garden was the size of a park. The penthouse had slippery floors and no garden for Poppy to play in when she was older, though Freya had assured Tara it was the perfect venue for parties.

'I'll introduce you to the staff,' Lucien murmured discreetly, 'and then I'd like you to get Poppy settled in as quickly as you can—'

'Of course…' Tara's brow puckered, she was thinking that Lucien seemed in quite a hurry to move things along. Cut him some slack, she told herself firmly. He was being considerate. He knew how tired they must be. It had been quite a day for him, as well.

Adjusting Poppy's position in her arms so everyone could see her downy cheeks and tiny, deep pink rosebud mouth, Tara followed Lucien into the magnificent hallway.

The floor was a chessboard of black and white marble, and there were gilded cream, pink-veined marble columns reaching towards a vaulted ceiling far above their heads. Apart from the murmur of voices pitched at a discreet level, there was a stillness and even a majesty to their surroundings. She had never been anywhere quite like it, Tara thought in wonder, though she had seen similar palaces in books, of course. The ornate painted ceiling was like something out of the Sistine Chapel. It had obviously been restored quite recently, and the colours were luminous—aquamarine, cobalt blue, ivory and cream, soft rose and peach tones...

'Shall I take Poppy from you?' Lucien offered.

Tara was still gawping open-mouthed at the ceiling and quickly collected herself. 'No, that's okay, thank you.' Instinctively, she tightened her hold on Poppy when Lucien made as if to take their baby niece out of her arms.

'I'll introduce you to the staff, then,' he said.

She was full of concentration now, wanting to remember everyone's name, but there were so many people to meet, it was inevitable she lost track eventually. The line stretched right across the hall.

It would take this many people to care for such a large building, Tara reasoned. She would just have to seek out each member of staff in private later. She wanted to introduce herself properly and get to know everyone so she could reassure herself about the people who would be caring for Poppy.

After the introductions had been completed, Lucien led their small party to the foot of the sweeping staircase. 'Now you will let me take Poppy,' he insisted. 'These marble steps can be quite dangerous when you're not used to them.'

Tara's gaze tracked up the towering staircase. He was right. She couldn't afford to take any chances with Poppy, she concluded, handing over her precious cargo.

They mounted the stairs beneath a legion of stern-faced ancestors. An older woman with grey hair, dressed in a sober uniform was waiting to greet them on the first landing. This was the housekeeper, Tara learned. She looked kind, Tara thought hopefully.

'Refreshments for the ladies?' Lucien checked with her before moving on down the wood-panelled corridor.

'*Oui*, Monsieur, le Conte,' the housekeeper confirmed, bobbing a curtsey to him. 'Everything is ready,' she said, sparing a warm and reassuring smile for Tara.

If she had needed any more reminders of Lucien's exalted position in life, she was sure to get them here, Tara reflected wryly as she smiled back.

'This is the nursery,' Lucien said, handing Poppy back so he could open a heavy wooden door. He stood back to allow Tara to enter in front of him. 'I hope you approve…'

Approve? Tara's eyes widened. She only wished Poppy was older so they could explore it together. This was only the sitting room, she gathered, seeing more doors leading off. She walked deeper into the inviting well-lit space, noticing that everything a baby could possibly need appeared to be, if not in place, then in boxes, and everything had been sourced from the very best of stores. It was a dream of a room, decorated in shades of rose-pink and ivory, cosy and yet not too small. There was a beautifully polished wooden floor topped with a deep rug, and comfortable sofas and lots of book shelves. Some of the child-friendly furniture was still covered in the protective wrapping which must have been used to protect it during delivery, but she could see the potential. 'It's fabulous,' she exclaimed excitedly. She couldn't wait to start organising it.

'It's not quite finished,' Lucien admitted. 'But I think everything's here. If there's anything more you need—'

Tara just shook her head, smiling. 'I'll be sure to let you know,' she told him happily, but even as she was thrilled by the preparations he had made, something in Lucien's eyes evoked a *frisson* of alarm inside her, as if everything wasn't quite as it appeared.

'I thought it better to wait for the nanny to tell the staff how she would like things arranged,' Lucien explained.

And he made that explanation a little stiffly, Tara thought. Was Lucien trying to shut her out, or was his remark simply a result of his upbringing? She could imagine that when you had grown up in such grand surroundings and had your every wish anticipated by an army of staff, you would have a different mind-set to someone brought up in an orphanage, but she wanted him to know that she intended to get stuck in and do her share of the work. 'But I'm here now,' she pointed out, 'so you don't have anything to worry about.'

Lucien's 'Hmm,' was hardly reassuring.

He turned to Liz. 'And this is your room for the duration of your stay,' he explained to the young nanny, walking across the room to open another door.

Tara smiled to hear Liz's gasp of delight. Who could

blame her? The room was very prettily decorated, with gingham curtains and a bed dressed with cream lace and a bank of coral-coloured velvet cushions.

'I had an interior decorator fit it out,' Lucien explained. 'I hope it's satisfactory.'

'With the addition of a waste bin and a mirror, it will be just perfect—' Seeing Lucien's face, Tara wished she could keep her sensible self under wraps sometimes. 'I'm sorry; I didn't mean to—'

'I'm sure Liz will find what she needs in one of those boxes out there,' Lucien said, cutting across her.

Once again, Tara got the feeling she was being shut out. 'Don't worry,' she told Liz discreetly, realising the young girl must be tired. 'I'll help you sort it out. It's only a small thing,' she added, turning to reassure Lucien.

Seeing a muscle flex in his jaw brought the uncomfortable feeling back again full force. She told herself she was tired too, and threw herself into sharing Liz's excitement. The room was beautifully presented and carefully colour-coordinated, with natural oak floorboards washed with white and covered with a fluffy rug. There were so many cute accessories they could start a store, the two girls agreed, laughing happily together. It looked just like something out of a magazine. Which, in a way, it was, Tara realised. Liz's bedroom was more like a set than a room to live in.

She kept these thoughts to herself as they toured an amazing pink marble bathroom, and both girls gasped when Lucien took them into Poppy's bedroom. There was a white cot set up on a platform carpeted with thick white fur, and the canopy over the cot was draped with a drift of white lace that trailed down the steps and was trimmed with pink satin ribbons. Tara and Liz exchanged a glance. It was fabulous, but had clearly not been designed by anyone who was used for caring for children. It would be all too easy to trip on the fabric as you carried a baby down the steps.

Not to worry, Tara told herself. She and Liz would soon rearrange everything. They would even find somewhere safe to display the beautiful lace so that Lucien would know they appreciated it. At least there were lots of shelves on which to arrange the toys and books, and there were even musical instruments for Poppy to play when she was older. Her modest home would fit here twice, Tara thought with amusement. Most importantly, how could Poppy not be happy here? How could anyone not be happy here?

How could she not be happy here?

She brushed that thought aside right away. She was here to scout the arrangements Lucien had made for Poppy, and nothing more. But still…

'Have your tea,' Lucien said gruffly, 'and then we'll go—'

'Go?' The *frisson* was back again, only now it was a full blown quake of alarm. Lucien had gone to a lot of trouble, Tara reasoned, and maybe he thought she had been too lukewarm. He would expect a better reaction from her when he showed her the room she was to have. 'The main thing is to see Poppy clean, fed and settled,' she reminded him. 'And then I'll help Liz sort everything out. You don't have to stay,' she assured him, knowing he must be tired too. 'I'm sure someone will show me my room…' She fell silent. Lucien wasn't just tense now, he was glowering at her. But what had she done? Drawing Poppy close, she brushed a kiss across her sleeping brow.

Lucien frowned as he watched her. 'I realise it's been a long day for you—'

'And for you too, and for Liz—' Tara exchanged an understanding look with the young nanny.

Lucien turned for the door. 'The internal phone's on the desk. Let me know when you're ready and I'll have someone drive you over—'

She was still smiling at this point. 'Drive me over?'

'To the gatehouse,' Lucien explained. 'In fact, you could leave now and have your tea there. I'll send someone up here to help Liz. Well, she seems to have everything in hand here,' he added when Tara looked at him.

She wasn't hearing straight, Tara concluded, calling on her sensible inner self to calm the alarm inside her. 'There's a lot to do,' she pointed out. 'I can't just leave Liz to get on with it.'

'She'll have help.'

Lucien was growing impatient. And she was guilty of selective hearing. What was it he'd said about a gatehouse? 'Do you mean I'm to go somewhere else?' Her anxious gaze flickered around.

'Why don't you give Poppy to Liz now?' Lucien said.

Tara became aware of Liz hovering on the sidelines while the housekeeper silently poured tea. It was like a film she was watching and yet wasn't a part of, she thought, feeling panic rise in her throat. But she mustn't make a scene—not here, in front of Poppy.

'Would you take Poppy for her bath?' she said in a voice that was only slightly shaky as she handed Poppy over to Liz. 'And make sure you have something to eat too—'

'I will,' Liz said, glancing worriedly at Lucien.

The housekeeper spoke up. 'I'll look after your young friend for you, *mademoiselle*.'

'Thank you…' There was nothing else for her to do, Tara realised as the two women left the room with Poppy. She felt sick and uncertain. 'Lucien, what's going on?'

'Poppy's my niece, part of my family, and as such she will stay here at the castle with me. You will only be a short drive away—'

'A short drive away?' Tara repeated foolishly.

'That's right,' Lucien confirmed.

'You mean you're keeping me from her?'

Lucien shifted position impatiently. 'Don't be so melodramatic. I've just explained to you, you'll only be a short drive away—'

'I'm not going anywhere unless Poppy and Liz come with me. Poppy doesn't know you.' As Lucien's eyebrows shot up, Tara firmed her chin. She might be at a disadvantage here, but both Liz and Poppy were in her care.

'For the sake of propriety, you must—'

'For the sake of propriety?' Tara's voice rose. 'The rules of propriety didn't seem all that important to you back at the hotel,' she reminded him frigidly.

'Please don't make this any harder than it has to be.'

Lucien's eyes were as hard and as cold as she'd ever seen them. His decision was made—had been made— and for some time, she gathered.

'You can see Poppy any time you like while you're staying in Ferranbeaux—'

Everything in Tara railed against Lucien's actions. 'If I ask your permission first, I presume?' She had always known her time with Poppy in Ferranbeaux would be limited, but she had not expected Lucien to tear them apart without warning her first.

'You only have to call me—'

'And if you don't happen to be in?' There was a

shake in her voice she couldn't control now. The end had come so suddenly. How could she abandon Poppy? How did she know Lucien would treat Poppy as she deserved? Would he be too busy to notice if Liz felt trapped and isolated in a big old castle peopled by servants? Was this it? For ever?

'For goodness' sake, Tara,' Lucien snapped, seeing her face, 'try to be grown up about this—'

'Grown up? Or detached?' she demanded in a voice that cracked with emotion.

Lucien answered her emotional outburst with silence.

'Why are you punishing me? What have I done to you?' Clinging to her last hope of staying close to Poppy, she was determined to reach him somehow. 'Treating me like this won't bring Guy back—'

'Don't you dare speak to me about my brother—'

'Why not, Lucien? Am I not *fit* to do so?'

His eyes blazed a warning, which she ignored. 'I know how deeply you loved your brother, even if you can't bring yourself to admit it.' She stood her ground as Lucien advanced a menacing step closer. 'Guy needed you—'

Lucien eyes blazed with a deadly intensity. 'What do you know of this? And why do you think I should want to talk about it now?'

'Because I want to make you feel something...' She pressed her lips together, and when she realised she wasn't getting anywhere, she exclaimed with exasperation, 'You cruel, hard man...can't you see what you're doing to yourself?'

Shaking her head, Tara looked at him sadly. 'And you ask me what I know of Guy.' Encouraged by his silence, she went on, 'I know that your brother and my sister took drugs—'

Lucien cut her off. 'That was common knowledge after the inquest.'

She waited until he was silent again. 'Guy and Freya's so-called friends were as bad as they were, and there were dealers coming round to the apartment all the time. Do I have to go on, Lucien? Or do you know what happened to your brother's fortune?'

'I have some idea,' he said coldly.

'You knew?' The thought horrified her.

'Of course I didn't know at the time. I was too busy rescuing the business and the estates Guy had declined to take an interest in to know what was happening at home. I only found out when Guy died and all the vultures started circling—'

'But you must have known Guy was weak—'

'Perhaps you knew him better than I did,' he snapped back viciously.

'So you still think I slept with him?' Laughing a sad little laugh, Tara shook her head in disbelief.

'Do you deny it?'

'Of course I do. And, from a purely practical point of view, the drugs had taken such a hold, I doubt Guy was capable of sleeping with anyone. Have you ever seen anyone on drugs, Lucien, scratching and sweating as they wander aimlessly about, waiting for their dealer to deliver?'

'If it was so bad, you could have contacted me—'

'Do you think I didn't try?' Grabbing her head in frustration, Tara finally lost her composure. 'Your secretary would never put me through to you. It was only when Guy and Freya were killed you decided to acknowledge my existence at all. Two years, Lucien,' she reminded him tensely as he stared coldly at her. 'Two years you ignored me. And now you can't keep away from me. Well, can you?'

He wasn't about to be trapped into an admission of that sort. And now he was locked in the past, reviewing his actions and each conversation he'd had with a brother he had thought he knew so well. 'When Guy refused the title and accepted the money—'

'What, Lucien? What?' she demanded as he murmured these thoughts out loud. 'What did you think? That Guy was being noble?'

'He didn't always come to the phone when I called him—'

She laughed again, but it was an ugly sound. 'And you want to know why that was, Lucien?'

He focused on her face, concentrating on the woman who had probably known his brother better than he had. 'Why don't you tell me?'

'Guy was most probably soiling himself, Lucien!'

And, as he sucked air through his teeth, thinking no new revelation could cause him more pain, she proved him wrong.

'And who do you think cleaned that up, Lucien?'

'Stop!' he commanded.

'Why? Because the truth is unpalatable? Or because you can't bear to hear it from me?'

He grabbed hold of her with an angry growl, then let her go. Could this be true? He didn't want to believe what she had told him, but that wouldn't make it go away. And now a part of him was remembering snatches of conversation and voices in the background when he had managed to get Guy on the phone… And then there was the money he'd loaned to Guy when common sense should have told him that Guy must have plenty of money of his own. He had put it down to Freya's excesses. Only when Guy was dead had he learned the truth.

'And you want to part me from Poppy when I've kept her safe all this time. How can you say you don't trust me, Lucien?'

She had made it hard for him to dismiss her as harshly as he had before. After what she'd told him he wished he'd been there for her, but it was too late for regret now.

'So that's why you're sending me to the gatehouse while you keep Poppy here with you?'

Her eyes were wounded, but she was no more, no less wounded than he was. What she had told him about Guy had cut him to the core, and if it was true he would never forgive himself.

'What do you suggest?' he demanded coldly.

'That I stay with her—'

And, before he could counter that, she added, 'In the servants' quarters, if that makes things easier for you—'

Easier for his conscience, did she mean?

'I wouldn't mind, Lucien.'

'And the staff wouldn't think it strange?' he demanded cuttingly, though guilt plagued him at the thought that she would do just about anything to stay with the baby.

'Do you care what anyone thinks?'

'It would only make things worse.'

'For whom, Lucien?'

So should he consign Poppy's aunt to the attic rooms, or stick her away in the gatehouse? The Count of Ferranbeaux was never at fault, Lucien reflected, hating himself at that moment—or, at least, he must never appear to be so. And those long-harboured suspicions that Tara might have slept with Guy had just received a mortal blow.

When he looked at Tara this time it was through different eyes and he saw how tired she looked. There were dark circles beneath her inexpertly made-up eyes—eyes that were brimming with tears—tears he'd put there. He didn't think he could feel any worse until he thought about Guy... Poor, poor Guy...

Oh, yes, he was proud of himself.

She had no energy left to fight Lucien. She was completely drained after letting go of all the tragic memories. If she could have helped Guy she would have done, but Guy hadn't wanted anyone's help. As Lucien went on staring at her, Tara knew what she must look like. She had provided him with entertainment at the hotel, but she wasn't stupid enough to think those events had any currency here. She didn't want them to have any currency, because whatever had happened between them, on her part, at least, had been driven by love. She could only throw herself on Lucien's mercy now.

'If I did stay in the servants' quarters...' his face didn't flicker, which gave her the courage to carry on '...do you promise you'd let me see Poppy first thing every morning?' Her heart sank as he turned away. 'Lucien?' How pathetically desperate she must sound, but she would fight for Poppy until the last breath left her body.

'You could come here each morning from the gatehouse,' Lucien pointed out, still keeping his back turned to her. 'There's a park beyond the courtyard where you could push the pram...' With an angry sound, he abruptly stopped speaking and raked his hair. 'They used to be jousting fields—' His face as he whirled around to stare at her contained more passion than she'd ever seen in him.

'I wouldn't take advantage of your hospitality. Ferranbeaux is Poppy's heritage. I know that. I also know you're not a charitable organization—'

'Good of you to notice.'

'I'll pay my way, Lucien.'

The flicker of humour in his eyes held no warmth.

'So, can I stay?' she persisted.

'*If* you stay,' he grated out, 'you will abide by my rules. There will be no more outbursts, and you will confide in no one—'

'Other than you, of course?' She met his gaze steadily.

'I'm not a bully, Tara—'

'And I'm not a doormat.'

'Just try to keep your thoughts to yourself. Well?' he demanded when she didn't answer immediately. 'Do you want to stay here or not?'

'Thank you for your gracious invitation,' she said quietly, careful to keep her face deadpan. 'I'd love to stay.'

Now what had he done? Tara living under the same roof was the very last thing he wanted. Conscious of the fragile state of his family name after all the troubles, he had planned to house her in the gatehouse—if she stayed in Ferranbeaux at all. After the newspaper reports, he had truly believed she had grown into the type of woman who would pocket his cheque and leave Ferranbeaux as fast as her legs could carry her. The cheque was still in his breast pocket, he confirmed, patting it. He had forgotten all about it. She had made him forget it. He had massively underestimated Tara, but then he had also underestimated the effect she would have on him after two long years apart. And why was he surprised by her stand now, after the way she had rallied at the press conference? She had earned herself a second chance.

'I'll ask the housekeeper to make a room ready for you.'

'If you're sure it's not too much trouble—'

There was no suggestion of sarcasm in her voice, and he wasn't sure if what he was about to say was an instruction or a vain hope. 'No trouble.'

She gave him a faint smile of acknowledgement. She had parried each thrust with dignity, using mostly calm reason and steady determination, though there had been a flash of that passion he so admired in her. She stared right back at him when he looked at her now, and it took quite a force of will to remind himself that however appealing he found her, there was no place for Tara in his life.

CHAPTER NINE

DECIDING to let the dust settle, Lucien returned to the
nursery after what he considered to be a reasonable
period of time to find Tara with the nanny in Poppy's
bedroom. They were busily reorganising the furniture,
while Poppy slept soundly in her Moses basket. He
noted the ornate cot had been stripped of all its decora-
tion and moved closer to the wall.

'I have people who will do that for you,' he pointed out.

'But we don't need them,' Tara told him. 'Do we, Liz?'

The young girl, looking much reassured now Tara
had returned, laughingly agreed, leaving him with little
more to do other than check everything was safe before
saying to Tara, 'A suite of rooms has been reserved for
you.'

'A suite of rooms?' she exclaimed. Lowering the table
the two girls had been carrying to the floor, Tara planted
her capable hands on her hips. 'Please tell your staff not
to go to any trouble for me. A small bedroom is all I
need—'

In spite of his fabled self-control, his lips tugged up
at that. 'Unfortunately, we don't do small here—'

'Uh-huh?'

She was mocking him, but in a nice way. Making her happy and more confident was both good and bad. His intention had never been to make her miserable, but he didn't want her getting her feet under his table either. 'Could you leave that for a moment? We need to talk. I'll send someone up to help Liz with the rest of it.'

Having checked with Liz, she agreed.

He took her into the sitting room and shut the door. Her cheeks had turned a deeper shade of rose with all the physical activity. He couldn't help thinking about the last time he'd seen her look so flushed.

'So?' She held out her hands as if waiting for his words of wisdom to drop into them.

He refused to be hurried. She looked relaxed, which transformed her. He felt reassured about his decision to keep her here, which transformed his inner state of mind. He studied the golden hair flying wildly round her face and noticed strands of it clinging to her forehead. She brushed them away. 'So, you'll settle for a suite?' he said dryly.

'Anything your housekeeper can arrange for me at such short notice I'm more than grateful for,' she told him candidly.

He didn't want her to be grateful. He wanted what a few hours ago he would have believed impossible, which was an ideal world where they were on equal terms and he could feel…anything. He hadn't bargained for a woman descending on him who, having assumed responsibility for her niece, had no intention of letting go without a fight. Tara had surprised him when she'd found fault with the ferociously expensive arrangements he had made for Poppy's arrival, but he was ready to accept she might be right about the practicalities that seemed to have escaped the notice of his interior decorator. As his frown deepened, she spoke up, no doubt with the intention of reassuring him.

'If it hadn't been for Poppy, I would have been happy to stay in the gatehouse—'

'If it hadn't been for Poppy,' he reminded her dryly, 'you wouldn't be here.'

She raised a brow at this brutal account of the truth, and when she levelled that turquoise gaze on him he thought her even more appealing.

'I realise this can't be easy for you, Lucien.'

'What can't?' he rapped, trying not to find the way she angled her face to speak to him quite so attractive.

'You've only heard such bad things about me,' she carried on, undaunted. 'And now, here I am, living in your house.'

'My castle,' he corrected her dryly.

'Your home, surely?' she prompted him quietly.

'Anyway, I'd like to thank you,' she said, before he had chance to dwell on it. 'I just want you to know I appreciate your generosity of spirit.'

He kept his face carefully under control. She was so young, and seemed so sincere, and as she brushed her hair from her face again it was such a childish gesture it made him long to reach out and sample the silky texture for himself. It wouldn't take much to throw them back onto a darker path than this one. He wanted her now.

'Your suitcase should have been delivered to your suite by now. If you need any help unpacking it–'

'Let me guess,' she interrupted, 'I only have to call downstairs and someone will come to help me.'

'That's right,' he said, thumbing the stubble on his chin.

'I don't think I'm the type of guest you're used to. I

don't have a lot with me. I doubt I'll need help with one change of clothes and a toothbrush.'

As she stared at him he couldn't help thinking that she was changing before his eyes. He could see the woman she would become, given half a chance.

The housekeeper chose this moment to interrupt them, saying that Tara's room was ready for her occupation. As he watched them talking together he thought the older woman and Tara might have been friends of long-standing to see them laughing and so relaxed. He had never seen his stern-faced housekeeper unbend like this before, but then, he reasoned, Tara's *joie de vivre* was infectious.

She wondered if Lucien was growing impatient with her. She was keen to meet his staff. She could tell they thought a lot of him, and she was eager to get to know them all by name so she could talk to them easily and understand the role they played in Lucien's household. She might not be staying for long, but she was looking to the future when Poppy would be cared for by these same people. So far she felt reassured. The people who worked for Lucien were different from those who had worked for Guy and Freya. Tara had secretly thought they must have had to sit some examination in snootiness before Guy would consider them, but there was no hint of pretension here.

Wanting to thank him for his change of heart, she caught up with Lucien at the door. Her heart thundered as he stared down at her. Was she seeing what she wanted to see, or was that another thread of warmth in his gaze? Would it disappear if she gave him another list of enquiries about his household? After all, she'd only just arrived.

'Don't,' he murmured as he opened the door.

What did that mean? Don't push it? Don't thank him? What? He didn't give her a chance to ask him. She would have to draw her own conclusions, Tara realised as the housekeeper approached.

'Are you ready, *mademoiselle*? Shall I take you to your room now?'

'Oh, yes, please…'

'Monsieur le Conte has asked me to tell you that he will be in his private apartment should you need him— and, of course, if you require anything more for yourself, or for Poppy and her nanny, please don't hesitate to call me.'

'Thank you, you're very kind,' Tara said sincerely, exchanging a smile with the housekeeper as she followed her out.

Tara thought she'd seen everything, but when the heavy oak door that marked the entrance to her suite of rooms swung open she gasped. The richness of everything was overwhelming and far too much to take in at a glance. She tried to concentrate on one thing at a time as the housekeeper gave her the guided tour, but she wasn't used to so much space, or so many *objets d'art* all together in once place, let alone such quantities of antique furniture, all of which was burnished to a mellow shine, leaving the faint scent of beeswax in the air. There were fabulous silk curtains at the windows in tones of kingfisher-blue and gold, and on the walls brocade in the palest yellow ochre, punctuated with gilt-framed mirrors and oil paintings showing ravishing beauties in flowing gowns, some of whom wore tiaras, while others sported wide-brimmed hats trimmed with feathers. The pretty rug on the polished wooden floor had to be Aubusson, Tara guessed, judging by the intricate floral design...And this was only the ante chamber to her bedroom, she discovered, as the housekeeper led her through to a second room where a large bed set in the centre of the room on a raised platform dominated.

The hall had been cosy, but all the other rooms seemed to be on such a grand scale she could only think that Guy and Lucien must have been lost inside them as small boys. She was already picturing them dressed by their nanny in miniature versions of their papa's silk dressing gown and pyjamas, with their hair neatly slicked back and monogrammed slippers on their tiny feet. Had the boys come downstairs to bow low and share a few stilted words with the Count before bedtime? If so theirs must have been a lonely and uncomfortable childhood not dissimilar to her own in many ways, Tara reflected, running her hand thoughtfully across the silk counterpane.

'Do you like the bed, *mademoiselle*?' the housekeeper enquired, reminding Tara that she was still staring at it.

'It's absolutely fabulous,' she said honestly, pulling her hand away, 'but do you think I could have some more pillows?'

'*Mais, certainement, mademoiselle*...certainly...'

The housekeeper probably thought she was mad. There was a bank of pillows three deep on the bed already, but the ornate sofas and chair looked so uncomfortable. And she had plans. Lots of plans. And those plans involved cushions and throws, and everything she could think of to make things more comfortable and homely while she was here.

'There are flowers in the garden, and in the hothouse, *mademoiselle*… But we weren't sure you would like them…'

'I'd love them!' Tara exclaimed. 'Thank you. And some for the Count too—'

'The Count, *mademoiselle*?' The housekeeper frowned.

'Oh, sorry, does he have an allergy?'

'Not to my knowledge, *mademoiselle*…'

'Then definitely for the Count and some for the nursery too. If you show me where I'm allowed to pick, I'll arrange them myself so I don't put you to any trouble.'

'It's no trouble, *mademoiselle*,' the housekeeper said, smiling at Tara's enthusiasm. 'Is there anything else I can do for you?'

'Do you have a handyman?'

'A handyman, *mademoiselle*?'

'To fit childproof locks for when Poppy is older, and to build fireguards. I've noticed all the open fires.'

'The Count prefers them.'

Then the Count was going to have to adapt to the new regime a small child would inflict on his household, Tara thought.

'We should have thought of these things in advance of your arrival,' the housekeeper said with concern.

'It's early days yet,' Tara reassured the older woman with a smile. 'I just want to be sure before I leave…'

'Yes, *mademoiselle*,' the housekeeper said gently as Tara's voice tailed away. 'Please try not to worry, *mademoiselle*…' And as their gazes met and held, the housekeeper touched Tara's arm. 'I can tell already that you're going to make a great difference here.'

Tara kept her feelings on that one to herself.

'This is my favourite guest room in the whole house,' the housekeeper confided.

'I'm not surprised.' Tara laughed, taking in the grandeur.

'And the Count is right next door...'

Ah. Tara's smile dimmed. 'Thank you,' she said quickly. 'I'm sure I'll soon find my way around.' It occurred to her then that perhaps the staff thought she wanted to be close to Lucien, and she couldn't cause any more disturbance for them than she already had by asking to be moved.

The housekeeper showed her the luxurious bathroom made for two, and Tara's cheeks burned red when she spotted the twin robes hanging on the bathroom door, and by the time she had been shown round the dressing room with its selection of silk robes and jewelled slippers all her pleasure in the suite of rooms had vanished and she was mortified.

'In case you've forgotten yours,' the housekeeper said lightly, as if there was nothing unusual in stocking such items in a guest suite. 'And if you need anything more you only have to ring down.'

'I'm sure there's everything I need right here.' Remembering her manners, she thanked the house-keeper. Did Lucien make a habit of this sort of thing? She was growing angrier by the minute.

'The Count wants people to have luxury during their stay...'

'He does?' How many of Lucien's house guests wore jewelled slippers?

'His father was just the same,' the housekeeper confided. 'It's considered part of the old world charm.'

Hmm, Tara thought.

'Well, I'll leave you to settle in.'

She would never wrap her mind around the sort of life Lucien led. But there was no point fretting about it. She was here and had to get on with it. Or she could always stay in her room and skulk in the shadows, a technique she had perfected over the years, and which had got her precisely nowhere to date. Besides, her curiosity was beginning to get the better of her. There was nothing to stop her finding out what all these sophisticated guests wore when they came to stay at the castle. She'd take a shower first, and then find out.

Having dried her hair, she cleaned her teeth and threw on a baggy top. Brushing her hair and twisting it into a no-nonsense knot, she could hardly wait to visit the Aladdin's cave that was her dressing room. But, of course, she was only going to look…

Oh…but this was rather nice…

Rifling through the rail of fabulous lingerie in the dressing room, Tara came across a robe exactly the same colour as her eyes. Deciding it wouldn't hurt to slip it on, she tugged off her top and carefully slid her arms into the diamante-sprinkled silk. What an exquisite experience that proved to be! The delicate fabric felt incredible against her skin. She inhaled with pleasure imagining the beauty who might wear it. When she finally plucked up the courage to look in the mirror, Lucien walked in.

'Oh, I'm sorry,' he exclaimed brusquely. 'No one could find you. I never imagined you'd be in here…'

No, and she could see why not. She knew she looked ridiculous in a robe meant for someone slim and hastily tried to cover herself.

'It might be better if you wait outside…' Clutching

the robe around her, she stared at him miserably, but Lucien refused to take the hint.

'Why don't you try this?' Searching expertly through the press of garments, he extracted a velvet robe in the palest shade of blue, trimmed with a froth of white lace. It was breathtakingly beautiful. 'And these,' he said, dipping down to retrieve what looked to Tara like the most expensive feathered slip-ons on the face of the earth.

'How do you know my size?' she asked as Lucien placed the dainty slippers in her hand, but then she blushed at his expression. There wasn't much they didn't know about each other's body. But as she hopped in ungainly fashion round the dressing room, battling with feathered mules, and attempting to swap robes, Tara's insecurities mounted. 'I really wish you'd leave me to get on with this,' she exclaimed, knowing her face was as red as a beetroot.

'Why?' Lucien murmured with a look in his eyes she knew only too well.

CHAPTER TEN

'I DON'T know how you can ask why I would like you to leave,' Tara said with a frustrated shake of her head.

'What do you mean?' Lucien appeared genuinely bemused.

'You can see me,' Tara insisted.

'And?'

'What part of stupid, fat, clumsy me did you miss?'

He shrugged. 'I saw *you*—'

'If you needed any more proof that Guy wouldn't want me...'

'Guy?' He frowned. 'I don't want to hear any more about Guy in connection with you.'

'You don't?'

'*I* wanted you.' He said this with a flash of the old humour, though his use of the past tense was hardly reassuring.

'And now?'

'I've seen you wearing fewer clothes than you're wearing now.'

'So you do believe me about Guy?'

'The only thing I don't understand,' Lucien admitted, as they were both clearing the air, 'is why Freya would say those things about you.'

'I've wondered about that too. It was only later I realised how frightened she must have been.'

'Freya, frightened?' Lucien clearly found that incredible.

'If Freya had lost Guy, she believed she would have nothing,' Tara explained. 'Freya knew Guy talked to me sometimes and that threatened her. Freya couldn't believe a man could look at a woman without there being sexual overtones. She didn't see what I saw...'

'Which was?' Lucien's eyes narrowed as he pushed for more information.

'In Guy's sick mind, drugs made things appear perfect until he came down again into his self-imposed hell. Guy wasn't just addicted to drugs, he was addicted to perfection and, well, I could never be that, could I?'

Tara said this so matter-of-factly that he was desperate to reassure her, but before he had a chance to do that she let the clothes in her arms drop and stood in front of him, completely vulnerable. 'I felt sorry for your brother, Lucien, and I tried—believe me, I tried. But Guy didn't want anyone to help him, least of all me. Why would he?' she pressed when he continued to stare at her. 'Well, look at me,' she insisted. 'I never even registered on Guy's sexual radar.'

He realised he was still standing rigidly like a fool, with his eyes narrowed as if Tara were talking to him in the one language he didn't understand. But he did understand how she must be feeling, and felt a wave of shame creep over him to think that anyone could have made her feel this way. Scooping up the discarded robe, he shook it out and handed it to her. 'Here—put this on. I'll turn my back...'

She didn't move to take it and, realising she didn't

want to move because she was so ashamed of her body, he unzipped it and went to her. With the same care as he might have dressed a child, he lowered it over her head.

Tara kept her eyes tightly shut. Was this the nicest thing Lucien had ever done for her, or the kindest? When he stepped back, she quickly swept up her discarded clothes and folded them neatly, desperate for something to distract his attention from her body.

'Haven't you forgotten something?'

'Have I?' She turned to face him, flinching as he reached towards her. It was as if everything that had happened between them counted for nothing, and they were starting all over again from this horribly embarrassing moment. 'Oh, the zip...' Realising what had attracted his attention, she quickly did it up again with a blasé, 'How could I forget that?'

'Because you were upset?' Lucien's head tipped to one side as he regarded her.

He had changed his clothes and showered too, Tara noticed, finally pulling herself together both mentally and sartorially. Smart black trousers cinched with a Hermes belt... Hermes loafers on his naked feet and a sharp blue shirt that had probably been custom-made for him. Even in the fabulous robe he'd selected for her, and which actually fitted, she felt more than a little underdressed.

'Better now?' he said.

'I will be when you stop looking at me.'

'Something wrong with the way I'm looking at you?'

She had never liked being in the spotlight and she didn't like the way he made her feel. 'You make me feel so fat,' she confessed, looking away from too much virile perfection.

'Fat?'

'Yes, you know…wobbly bits.' Actually, he wouldn't know, Tara realised as she turned around to confront Lucien.

His lips tipped up. 'Actually, I like your wobbly bits.'

She was supposed to believe him?

'There's only one thing wrong…'

'Yes?' She was still acting defiant, but inside she had just been reduced to a snivelling bunch of insecurities.

'Let your hair down…'

'That's it?'

'Let your hair down,' Lucien repeated.

She reached up but, before she had a chance to take the clip out of her hair, Lucien had done it for her. As her hair bounced onto her shoulders he smiled. 'That's better,' he said.

'Are you sure that's it?'

'What else did you think I was going to say?'

If he thought she was going to give him more ammunition than could be gleaned by the evidence of his own eyes, he was wrong.

'You have to stop this, Tara. If I say you're beautiful I don't expect you to argue…'

'Beautiful?'

'Don't play the fool with me; we both know you're too smart for that.'

There was just enough warmth in Lucien's eyes to convince her he was being serious. It prompted her to ask the question she should have asked him the moment he'd come into the dressing room. 'Why are you here, Lucien?'

He continued to stare at her and the longer they held each other's gaze, the less his motive seemed to matter. If it had been anything urgent, he would have told her right away, Tara reasoned. 'Don't,' she said, flinching as he ran the knuckles of one hand very lightly down her arm.

'Don't?' he queried softly.

'Don't you know I'm exhausted?' she tempered. And even that was feeble when Lucien only had to look at her a certain way and she'd instantly recover from anything the day had thrown at her. And he was looking at her that way, Tara realised, lifting her eyelashes the smallest amount. 'Are you laughing at me?'

'I'm not laughing at you…'

No, but he was stroking her arm so tenderly it made it impossible for her to concentrate. 'Lucien, please…'

'Please what?' he teased in a husky voice. 'If you wanted to be alone you could have stayed at the gatehouse.'

'That's unkind…'

'Unkind?' Dipping his head, he stared into her eyes. 'Let me assure you that I only intend to be extremely persuasive, attentive and, ultimately, hugely satisfying…'

'Hugely satisfying…?' She sighed.

'That's right…'

This was the moment when she should reject him and play him for all she was worth, but that was another girl in another lifetime, and one who was much less in love than she was.

Lucien carried her into the bedroom, where he tossed back the sheets and laid her down on the bed. She barely had time to inhale the crisp clean scent of fresh air and sunlight rising from the bedding before he kicked off his loafers and joined her. Drawing her into his arms, he stretched out his length against her, and as his weight pressed into her she knew it wasn't her imagination telling her this was the safe harbour of her dreams.

Lucien's lips were a familiar and irresistible introduction to the pleasures in store for her, but he wouldn't be rushed. He wasn't in half as much hurry as she was, Tara concluded, but why would he be when the outcome was so certain? He felt so firm and warm and strong, and was everything she wanted him to be and more. She pressed against him greedily, but it wasn't enough; it could never be enough. She gasped with anticipation when he brought her beneath him, containing her with his powerful frame, and pacing her pleasure as his lips incited little flames of sensation all down her neck.

Capturing her wrists, he held them high above her head, resting them on the bank of pillows so he could enjoy kissing her as much as he wanted to without her interference. He had every intention of appreciating each glorious inch of Tara at a speed that suited him. That it suited Tara he had no doubt. Judging by her sighs and the way she writhed beneath him, she was enjoying it. She liked it even more when he whispered suggestions in Catalan, a language he knew she couldn't understand, though she certainly got his meaning. He loved the look in her eyes and he loved the way her robe fell apart, revealing all her lush perfection the moment he pulled down the zip.

'What an accommodating robe,' he murmured, stripping it away in one swift movement.

'You are…'

'Impossible?' he suggested. 'No.' He pressed against her, loving the way her cushioned form yielded beneath his hard muscled frame. If there was a more perfect woman on the face of the earth he had yet to meet her.

The more she pressed against him, the more Lucien answered her with those wicked words against her lips. She knew they were wicked even though she couldn't understand them. Why else would he have that look in his eyes? Why else would he be working his magic on her now? She loved this feeling of being safe in his arms, even when she was completely in his power. She loved the way he held her so firmly with one hand clasping her buttocks and the other securing her wrists. She could feel the shift of hard muscle beneath his smooth, tanned skin, and the power of his erection against her thighs. The way she felt now tempted her to believe she could have it all—Lucien and Poppy...a proper life, a proper family... And as he whispered her name against her neck she trembled with desire, and when he let go of her wrists she immediately captured him, linking her fingers behind his neck to drag him back to her.

'Kiss me,' she ordered him. Make me forget the truth of our situation, was what she meant. 'Kiss me,' she repeated fiercely.

Lucien made love to her so tenderly that emotion welled inside her. She hid it, of course, and was relieved when she was incapable of feeling anything other than the most intense pleasure imaginable. She was glad her breasts were so large—Lucien made her glad. She had worked out that girls with small breasts must receive proportionately fewer kisses, which led her on to wondering who would want to be thin. She'd worked all this out long before Lucien nudged his way between her thighs and if she had a complaint, it was that he seemed intent on taking her as if she were the most fragile thing on earth.

'If you stop now,' she warned him when he paused to lavish kisses on her belly, 'I swear I'll never forgive you...'

'Never forgive me this?' Lucien queried in the stern voice she loved above anything. Dipping his head, he delivered the most intensely pleasurable attentions with his tongue.

'Okay, I might forgive you that,' Tara conceded, gasping.

Lucien laughed the confident laugh of a man who knew his skills in bed came with satisfaction guaranteed. He was about to migrate down that bed when Tara dragged him back again. 'No,' she commanded, raising her hips seductively. 'You don't get away from me that easily…'

'What makes you think I want to?'

He pinned her to the bed with his weight and she responded exactly as he'd hoped she would. Whatever she said, Tara was the perfect woman. She would stay in Ferranbeaux. She would stay with him. She would see Poppy exactly as and when she wanted. As the mistress of Lucien Maxime, the Count of Ferranbeaux, who would stop her?

After their shower they returned to the sitting room in their robes. Tara settled on the rug in front of the fire, staring into it with a pensive expression on her face. With her knees drawn up to her chin and her hair lit by the firelight so it became a cloud of glittering gold to frame her face, she had to be the loveliest thing he had ever seen.

He went to hunker down beside her and, cupping his hand around her head, he drew her close. 'You're beautiful.'

'Don't be silly,' she said at once.

'I've never been more serious in my life…' He closed his eyes to allow his senses full rein. He could feel her soft curls springing against his palm, and inhaling her fresh warm scent he knew this was one of life's better moments. 'A much better moment,' he murmured, speaking his thoughts out loud.

'Sorry?' She turned to look at him.

'This is much better than fighting all the time, don't you think?' He nuzzled his chin against her neck and then realised she looked stricken.

When he pulled back, she said, 'Oh, Lucien, I'm so sorry I was brutal about your brother…'

'The truth is brutal.' And he was more concerned about Tara right now. Guy was beyond his help, but whoever had made Tara feel so self-conscious and worthless had given him a task he could do something about. Drawing her close, he kissed the top of her head. How could he convince her he'd never known such peace before? Just sitting with Tara resting against his chest in front of the fire was enough for him. But as he listened to the crackle of wood as the logs burned and shifted he felt his sleeve grow wet. 'Tara…?' When she didn't answer he held her closer still, determined to make everything right for her. But they came from different worlds, he reminded himself, and his was ruled by duty, so how did he intend to do that?

He decided she must be grieving for Freya, and instinct told him the best way to counsel her was to commune in silence so she knew he understood, and when she looked at him as if trying to read his deepest thoughts, he did the only thing that felt right to him.

As Lucien kissed her it was like the sun coming out after a storm, food after a siege. This was where she belonged. Lucien was everything to her and she gave herself to him again without reservation. The tenderness they'd shared over the past few hours was what had sustained her for two long years, and now he had come back to her…

So enjoy it while it lasts, the demon doubt inside her whispered spitefully.

CHAPTER ELEVEN

TARA woke at dawn the following morning to find
Lucien had already showered and left her, and there
was just a rumpled pillow and his indentation on the
bed. Gathering his pillow to her, she inhaled deeply,
wondering if she'd ever been so happy. They had turned
a corner, she was sure of it. And all her doubts? Were
left behind, she told her inner voice firmly.

After taking a shower, she dressed quickly in her old
jeans and a T-shirt and, after checking Poppy was still
asleep with Liz in the next room, she hurried downstairs
to find breakfast...and maybe bump into Lucien.

Tara's first impression of Lucien's home hadn't
changed as she walked downstairs. It was crying out for
some homely touches. She didn't like to think of Lucien
and Guy growing up here. She didn't like to think of
Poppy growing up here, come to that. Biting her lip with
concern, Tara glanced back up the stairs towards the
nursery. The castle of Ferranbeaux was like a wonderful museum, full of priceless objects that no one must
touch. But it wouldn't take a magic wand to turn it into
a home. Maybe the scent of age and great wealth was
omnipresent, but her imagination could easily conjure

up a time when the castle had been a family home. The pockmarked stone could be draped with warm-coloured hangings, and with a little tweaking here and there and some well-chosen pieces of furniture even the vast scale of the building would seem less daunting. There were so many lovely features—the magnificent staircase for one, with its smooth roll-topped banister. It made her think about all the hands that must have brushed the polished wood to a patina so fine it felt like polished silk. The light filtering in through innumerable panes of jewelled glass was absolutely magical, and with a few more well-placed lamps to eradicate the shadows… How she would love to share the renovation of it with Lucien.

And now she really was dreaming, Tara told herself firmly as she reached the bottom of the stairs.

'The Count is in the breakfast room, *mademoiselle*,' a servant murmured to her. 'Shall I show you?'

'Thank you…' Tara's heart leapt. Would she ever get used to being part of Lucien's life again?

When she walked into the dining room the addition of plaster dust on the front of Lucien's thighs where the denim had been stretched across hard muscle told her he'd already been out early that morning working on the renovations.

'Hello,' she said cheerily, sure he must know how she felt—as if all her Christmases had come at once.

'Good morning,' he said quite formally, barely looking at her.

She told herself that his reserve was for the servants hovering round them. Lucien would hardly want to announce to the world that they had spent the night together. When he suggested they take breakfast outside on the terrace she readily agreed, knowing this would give them a degree of privacy they couldn't enjoy in the dining room.

'Coffee?' Lucien said, once he'd seen her comfortably settled on an attractive cane chair with a deeply padded seat. 'Or tea?'

'Juice, please…' She smiled up at him. She could hardly wait to tell him what last night had meant to her. Just being here with Lucien brought the world into sharper focus, though he did still seem a little distracted.

And no wonder, Tara thought, gazing out across the raised terrace. The formal gardens were fabulous, prompting the thought that maybe someone had to clip the neat little box hedges with a pair of hand scissors one leaf at a time to achieve such a perfect outline. The scent of roses and lavender drifted on the same breeze that rippled the glassy lake…and, on that lake, swans glided elegantly, giving no hint as to the furious paddling going on beneath the smooth surface of the water to sustain their forward momentum. She felt a certain comradeship with those swans, Tara mused as Lucien sipped his coffee in silence. It was impossible not to compare the grandeur of the parkland surrounding Lucien's home to the narrow street and small cinder playground in front of her small house back home. Maybe that was why he'd brought her here, to let her see what she was up against…

It was a relief when the waiter wheeled a trolley over and she was forced to choose breakfast rather than dwell on the comparisons a court of law might make. When it came to access rights to Poppy, surely love counted for something? She had to believe it did.

'If you don't like anything on the trolley you can order something else,' Lucien told her.

'Thank you, this is fine.' Tara's heart squeezed tight. She could pretend all she liked, but the truth was they were back to square one. Last night had meant nothing to him, and that hurt her more than she could possibly have imagined. Even out here in the sunshine she was in the shadows, perhaps now more than ever. 'Lucien…'

First he waved the waiter away, and then, with a faint air of impatience, he turned to her. 'Yes? What is it, Tara?'

'I love you,' she whispered.

'I thought I'd show you the city today,' he said, leaning back in his chair as if she had just asked him to pass the salt. 'I think you'll want to see it to reassure yourself about where Poppy will be living—'

'Didn't you hear me?'

Thrusting his chair back, Lucien got to his feet. 'Let's take this inside, shall we?'

Did she have an alternative?

Lucien walked into his study and she followed.

He shut the door behind them.

'Lucien, I—'

'Just listen this time.' He held up his hands with a grim expression on his face. 'And, for once, please, don't speak—'

She couldn't speak. She couldn't believe he would speak to her like that.

'I don't…I can't…I have never loved,' he told her with a decisive gesture. 'And I'm not about to start now. It isn't your fault,' Lucien informed her stiffly. 'That's just how it is. So please don't talk to me about love, or bring it up again. If there's anything I've done to lead you on—'

'Just a minute,' Tara said quietly. 'Are you telling me you don't believe in love, and yet you're intending to adopt Poppy?' There wasn't a part of her that wasn't trembling as she asked the question. She was suffused with fear for the future of the little girl she loved so deeply, and hurt that Lucien could be so unfeeling towards her. In those few words he had made her feel used and dirty and stupid.

'Don't be ridiculous. Poppy will get everything she needs from me.' Tara's expression irritated him. It was as if she didn't believe him. She probably thought emotion was everything, whereas he knew for a fact it was a dangerous distraction. Closing himself off from emotion had brought him success in life, and it wasn't that hard to do. He just had to remember how it had felt to be rejected by the Count, his father. When he remembered how he had dealt with that, the rest was easy. He had never been an attention-seeker like Guy and so he had shut himself off as a child, killing off his ability to feel in the process. This time he was doing it for Tara rather than for himself. He would give her no false promises or lead her on in any way. His only regret was that he had allowed things to go this far. He was mid-self-congratulation when a waiter came in with a tray of breakfast. He often ate at his desk and his meals were brought to him without ceremony so he could continue working.

'Monsieur le Conte,' the man murmured, 'you left the table so I had the chef prepare something fresh for you…'

Which, he had to say, smelled delicious…

'Let me take it,' Tara offered.

He was relieved when Tara spoke up and not a little surprised to see how quickly she had regained her composure. He was glad she had taken their little talk so well. After last night he had been keen to set things straight between them at the earliest opportunity.

Satisfied that everything was back to normal, he settled down in his swivel chair. 'Just put the tray down on the desk for me, will you?' he said, clearing a space for it. 'What about some breakfast for you?' he asked as the waiter was about to leave. He noticed then that her face was ashen, and waved the man away. 'What's the matter?'

'You...you and Poppy,' she said in a quiet voice. 'You caring for Poppy—'

'We both care for Poppy—'

She shook her head. 'No, Lucien. By your own admission, you're not capable of caring for anyone.'

'I'm more than capable,' he assured her confidently.

'I should have known,' she murmured as if she hadn't heard him.

'You should have known what?'

She looked at him steadily then. 'I should have known that the man who left a small fortune on my bed after taking my virginity before disappearing from my life—'

'What did you say?' he demanded, suddenly acutely tuned in.

'I think you heard me. And don't feel guilty. There was no way you could possibly have known. It was my choice to do what I did that night, but I did think I might have heard from you afterwards. I didn't realise people could just shut themselves off. That night was special for me, and I thought it was for you—'

She had given him an opening, and paled when he said nothing. Getting to his feet, he considered what to say next. He had to achieve a balance between raising her expectations unfairly and crushing her. 'You're wrong to think that night meant nothing to me—'

'I don't know how you can say that, Lucien, when you never once made any attempt to contact me.'

'You know as well as I do that life intervened. I lost my brother—'

'And I lost my sister, and I have yet to hear one word of condolence from you. Why should I think that sleeping with me meant any more to you than scratching an itch?'

'Tara!'

'I don't see why you should sound so shocked. That's what you've reduced that night to. But where Poppy's concerned your cold-blooded approach isn't enough; she must have love.'

'And she'll have it—'

'From you?' Tara flinched as Lucien's blazing gaze dared her to say more. How startlingly attractive he was, and yet how cold. She was close enough to detect the scent of his soapy shower and to see that his hair was still damp and curling tenaciously round his cheekbones, but she had more sense than to stay around and let him work his magic on her once again. 'I won't keep you. There's nothing worse than cold eggs,' she said instead.

'We'll talk about this later,' he promised, turning his attention to his rapidly cooling breakfast. It was better to let her calm down, he reasoned.

'Let me save you the trouble,' she said in her usual non-combative tone and, before he knew what was happening, she had picked up his plate and tossed the contents in the bin. 'Enjoy!' she snapped on her way out of the room.

Tara sought refuge in the nursery. It was the only place she felt she belonged. Being with Poppy and doing the little tasks for the baby filled her with so much joy it went some way to scrubbing out the anger she felt where

Lucien was concerned. He was a lost cause, Tara decided, swishing the warm water in the baby bath over Poppy's chubby legs. Reaching for a towel, she wrapped it around the adorable warm, wriggly body and exchanged some baby noises with her niece as she lifted her. Then she felt Lucien's presence in the room. She turned to face him. He was leaning against the door, watching her. She stared back, telling him without words that he had no place being here unless he was prepared to respect the haven of a small baby and the woman who cared for her and loved her.

'I wondered if you'd like some breakfast, after all?' he said dryly.

'No, thank you. Would you like to hold your niece?' She advanced fearlessly, holding Lucien's gaze all the while.

'Me?'

'Why not? She's clean, and she's lovely. It's a great privilege, Lucien.'

He could see that. He reached for the baby. Seeing Tara holding Poppy had had an effect on him, leaving him warm and calm. He wasn't ready to let go of that yet.

Tara transferred his baby niece into his arms with the greatest care. As she looked at him a flash of understanding passed between them that said he had pushed her in the study and she had shoved him back. Tara had put her stake in the ground, and he could only respect that.

Holding the baby in his arms was an extraordinary feeling. He didn't want to let the little girl go, and could have stared into the depths of those sapphire eyes for a long, long time. He only wished Poppy was old enough for him to reassure her that he would care for her and protect her all his life and that he would even learn to

love, if she would show him. His gaze met Tara's over
the baby's head and she smiled at him. 'Why don't we
go out?' she suggested. 'It might do us all good to have
some fresh air…'

'Why don't we?' he said, surprising himself, and they
agreed to meet outside on the terrace in forty minutes.

She should have known Lucien would change his outfit
for a walk about in the city. He looked every bit the Count
in a crisp bone-coloured linen shirt, which he had teamed
with an elegant summer-weight jacket, beautifully
tailored trousers and nut-coloured designer loafers exactly
the same shade as his hair. Tara felt a little awkward at his
side in her jeans and simple top, but when she was with
young children she knew better than to dress up and, with
Lucien introducing her so warmly to everyone they met
as his niece's aunt, it wasn't long before she relaxed.

Plus Lucien had a position to uphold, Tara reminded
herself wryly as they walked along the cobbled streets
pushing Poppy in her buggy, while she most assuredly
didn't. The Count of Ferranbeaux was on show to his
people, she reasoned as he stopped to chat with some
men playing boules along the way. It was the first of
many encounters, and it was easy to see how proud the
people were of their Count—easy to see why they
would be, when Lucien looked every bit the aristocratic
with his proud features and his fabulous physique.
While he stopped yet again to exchange a good natured
conversation involving lots of hand gestures and excla-
mations, she excused herself politely and, pushing
Poppy into a nearby shop, she bought some ice cream.

'You didn't need to do that,' Lucien exclaimed when
she handed him a dripping cone.

'You carry money?' she challenged dryly. 'Or perhaps you're afraid of spilling some down your suit?'

Tipping his sunglasses down his nose, he gave her a look before settling them back in place again. 'I carry money,' he assured her, 'and I certainly don't have accidents.'

There was so much to see and now she was relaxed she was full of questions. Lucien brought everything in the city to life for her, and if there was a moment when his enthusiasm turned down a notch it was when he shared his disappointment at not finding an architect qualified to help him restore the rotunda of the ancient basilica. The circular tower required a specialist in medieval architecture, he told her, and to date his team had failed to find one who was sufficiently knowledgeable.

They moved on from the shopping area to a cypress-shaded avenue which Lucien told her was an alternative route back to the castle. Sunlight dappled the pavements and there were skylarks swooping back and forth. It was a picturesque area, and one of the oldest in the walled city, Lucien explained. There was even a small park here, Tara discovered, with a playground, and she found herself looking for signs that said, 'À Louer', meaning 'to rent', though she knew it was only a daydream. But perhaps she should start planning to find somewhere else to stay, because the next time she came to Ferranbeaux to see Poppy it might not be convenient for Lucien to have her stay at the castle.

CHAPTER TWELVE

LUCIEN invited her to eat dinner with him that evening. She had to keep a line of communication open between them, Tara reasoned as she took a shower. They still had a lot to talk about where Poppy was concerned.

And that was why her heart was pounding with excitement and her head was full of dreams…

Yes, well, she would put her sensible head on now, along with the only dress she'd brought with her, a modest cream shift with a pretty coral-coloured edging and a lacy cardigan to match. Slipping her bare feet into simple sandals, she made two very important phone calls before going down for dinner. The first went well, but the second, which involved her viewing and then potentially signing the lease for a room in an apartment building in the city, made her mad as hell. Women couldn't do that in Ferranbeaux, she was told. She must have the lease countersigned by a man.

What sort of place was this?

He had the shower turned to ice. The temperature of the water matched his mood exactly. He had shunned feelings all his life, only to have Tara break through his reserve. Turning off the water, he stepped out of the shower. Grabbing a towel, he dried off roughly. Had she turned down his invitation to stay at the gatehouse because she was playing for higher stakes? Was he guilty of drawing a veil over the fact that she was out of the same mould as Freya because he wanted her? With so many people depending on him, he couldn't afford to make the same mistake as Guy had with Tara's sister. The citizens of Ferranbeaux were waiting for him to take a wife not a mistress.

Guy had refused the title, Count of Ferranbeaux, because of the responsibilities that came with it. Lucien had taken on those responsibilities, knowing they would colour his actions for the rest of his life. He wasn't about to forget his duty to his countrymen now. Guy had been left the family money and so Lucien had always known he'd have to prove himself, which he had, and now he was going to use some of that money to complete the renovations his city so badly needed. Would he risk everything for Tara, when he wasn't one hundred per cent sure of her? He had schooled himself to believe his inclination where matters of the heart were concerned was a selfish indulgence and if he married at all it would be in the interests of his people. That determination had never changed. He would always put Ferranbeaux first.

Planting his fists on the cold hard marble, he stared into the mirror at a man he didn't like too much. Life had made him suspicious to the point where he couldn't see the good in people any longer. Guy's associates had turned his stomach with their tales of bills unpaid and promises his brother had made before his death. He'd paid them off to get rid of them, but it had left a bad taste in his mouth and a lingering mistrust of others that he couldn't seem to shake off…though this afternoon with Tara and Poppy had given him something more to think about. But he had inherited control of a region where antiquated laws prevailed, and he should be devoting all his energies to redrafting them rather than indulging in a dalliance with Freya's sister.

Tugging on his jeans, he pulled on a clean top and, ruffling his hair into order, he left the bathroom. This time with Tara had made him restless. She was no longer the ingénue he'd met two years ago, or even the same woman who had been waiting for him so anxiously at the hotel. She had come alive under pressure, and he was glad of it for her sake, but if she wanted to stay on in Ferranbeaux his terms for that were clear.

The desire to blow some fresh air through her muddled mind had gone badly astray, Tara concluded as she clung onto an icy metal upright. She hadn't expected the wind to be so strong out here on the castle ramparts. She had been lured onto a part of the walkway that was being renovated by the promise of an even better view over the walled city at night time, and was standing on some wooden planks over a drop she didn't even want to think about—especially not when the wood creaked every time the wind blew, and the wind blew all the time. She suddenly wasn't so sure she was brave about heights. She thought about Poppy, warm and safe in bed. She wouldn't be much use to Poppy if she fell, and the media would have a field day if she did. She had no option but to let go of the pole and start edging gingerly along. But the first step she took met with empty air and as she shrieked a voice called out—

'Don't move… I'm coming to get you…'

'Lucien…' Her hands were welded to the pole and she didn't dare to turn around, but she felt the wood shift when he stepped onto it. 'Is it safe for us both to be standing here?'

'What do you think?' he growled. 'I'm tempted to leave you here.'

'No—'

'Next time you feel like taking a stroll out here,' he said, wrapping an arm around her waist, 'call me first. Come on—you have to move.'

'Can't—'

'You must.'

Her throat was so dry she could barely form words. 'Lucien…'

'You have to trust me. There's a drop of around a hundred feet below us, so just do as I say for once.' He started peeling her fingers from the pole.

'Please—no…'

The rest of her protests were lost in a gasp as Lucien swung her into his arms. 'There are times to argue and this sure as hell isn't one of them.' Carrying her inside, he kicked the door shut behind them. 'Didn't you see the notices warning that this part of the building is unsafe?'

Having been dropped unceremoniously to her feet, Tara was not at her most complacent. 'It was dark—'

'Forgive me for not anticipating reckless guests. I'll have lanterns placed there.'

'Good idea,' she agreed, still shaking with fright.

'What were you doing out there, anyway?'

'I needed time to think—'

'More time?'

'Yes, more time, Lucien. There are quite a few things we need to iron out—'

'Like safety measures? You could have been killed out there.' He stood aside to let her pass but, as she did so, he caught hold of her and kept her trapped with his fists planted against the wall either side of her face. 'No more adventures, Tara—'

She was so sure he was going to kiss her she gasped as he pulled away.

'You don't need to walk across unsupported planks to prove how independent you are.'

She shook her head. 'That wasn't it at all.'

Lucien wasn't listening. She could see the strain in his face that told her how much danger she'd been in.

'I care about your safety.'

'I know, and thank you—'

'As I care about the welfare of all my people,' he said over her.

'But that's just it—I'm not your person, Lucien.'

He was still rocked by the thought of Tara plunging to her death, and was in no mood for lectures. 'Save your stand-alone principles for someone who gives a damn. There is such a thing as teamwork and cooperation—'

'Which you, of course, champion,' she flashed back. 'Am I the only one here who should learn to compromise? Can you compromise, Lucien? No,' she said after a moment, 'I didn't think so.'

'You don't have to break away from everyone to prove you're not like Freya,' he rapped, troubled by the thought that, even at her worst, Freya could never have evoked this level of feeling in him.

'And you don't have to be so hard to prove you're not like Guy—'

As silence rang between them he had more than enough opportunity to contemplate how uncomfortable the truth could be.

'Lucien… I'm so sorry… You almost certainly saved my life.'

He looked at her, wondering who was saving whom here. 'Just make sure you don't take risks like that again.'

This time Tara held her tongue. Would it have occurred to Lucien that just being in his company was the biggest risk of all?

Lucien insisted Tara must warm herself in front of the fire and have a hot drink, and she didn't argue when he led the way back to his apartment. She noticed more this time, now there was no red mist of passion to distract her. It was a man's space with no unnecessary items or even family photographs, which surprised her. She had expected one of the Count, his father, at least. No wonder Lucien had called on the services of an interior decorator to furnish the nursery. She guessed that, having been brought up in the formal splendour of a castle, he had no cluttered family home references to draw on. But at least he had chosen autumn-coloured textiles to soften the effects of wood and stone, and the furniture was all designed to be comfortable rather than stylish.

Having closed the outer doors behind them, he drew a soft gold curtain across them, shutting out the windy night. 'Sit,' he invited, gesturing towards one of the two taupe-coloured sofas arranged either side of a roaring fire.

The fire proved a stronger incentive and she went to kneel in front of it, wondering if she would ever thaw out. When a few minutes had passed, all the thoughts that had propelled her outside in the first place came to the forefront of her mind. 'What if I accepted your offer to stay at the gatehouse?' she said without turning round.

She heard Lucien shift position on the sofa and sensed his interest. 'I'd be delighted,' he said carefully in a way that told her he knew there was more to come.

'It seems inevitable I'll be staying on here in Ferranbeaux—at least until the final details of the adoption are ironed out…'

'Go on…'

'But if I stay at the gatehouse you must let me pay rent.'

'Rent?'

She turned to face him. 'What's wrong with that?'

Lucien frowned. 'You're my guest. I don't expect you to pay your way.'

'But if I want to?'

'No,' he said flatly.

'So what will I do?' She thought about the phone call and the tiny place she'd found that she couldn't even rent without Lucien's permission. 'You know, don't you?' she said, seeing the way he was looking at her.

'Do I know that you tried to rent a property in the city?'

'There isn't much you don't hear about, I imagine.'

Silence greeted this remark.

'So you also know I'd need you to countersign the lease before I can rent anywhere—'

'There are reforms I have yet to make,' he said pointedly.

'But would you sign?'

'Would I sign so you could live in poverty? What sense would there be in that?'

'I'd make it work—'

'But you don't have to.'

He didn't have to say another word. She already felt humiliated, and saw the irony in that at the very moment when Freya would have been inwardly dancing with triumph. 'So what's your suggestion, Lucien?'

'I think you know…'

No! Everything in her railed against it. It would never work between them, Tara realised, forcing back her grief. She could never, *never* do as Lucien wanted.

'Become your mistress?' she asked him bluntly. 'Live in the gatehouse, where I'm on hand if you should need me? Don't you think Freya's example taught me anything?'

'You don't have to walk in Freya's shadow all your life. It's up to you if you step out of it—'

'That's easy for you to say when you sacrifice nothing to do as you suggest—'

'What other solution is there?' Lucien cut across her. 'What's your suggestion, Tara?'

As he held her gaze she realised this was the end of her pathetic daydream. Sharing her life with Lucien and Poppy was never going to happen, and it was time for her to face reality. She loved Lucien with all her heart. She wanted him. She wanted to spend the rest of her life with him and Poppy, and Lucien was telling her she could only have the scraps. But she was done with accepting whatever life threw at her.

'Who are you, Lucien?' she demanded angrily. 'Who are you really? When did you grow to be so cold?' Tara flinched as she saw something inside him snap.

'Do you really want to know?' Lucien demanded coldly, making her squirm at the thought of what might unfold.

'Yes, I do,' she said.

She remained absolutely still, afraid to breathe or move in case he shut himself off from her again.

'I'm a bastard,' he told her. 'I'm the bastard son of the Count of Ferranbeaux. Are you satisfied now?'

His smile was all cruel irony, but she wasn't nearly satisfied and firmed her jaw, determined to learn whatever else he had to tell her. 'I thought you grew up here at the castle?'

'You thought wrong.' Lucien's tone was clipped—to conceal those feelings her persistence had unlocked, Tara suspected as his stare blazed down into her face. 'I grew up on the wrong side of the tracks with a mother who always put her rich bene-factor first. Don't feel sorry for me. It made me the man I am today—'

Lucien's short, humourless laugh made her flinch inwardly. 'I had no idea,' she admitted softly.

'That I was the son the Count discarded?'

Hearing the pain of long years' standing, she said not a word.

'Discarded until my father's legitimate heir turned down the title, that is—'

Understanding flooded her brain. Now she knew why Lucien was so cold. She realised how frightened he must have been as a child when showing his feelings would only guarantee more rejection. She felt compas-sion for that child and knew Lucien the man was a hostage for life to the duties he had taken over from those who least deserved his help.

'Ferranbeaux means everything to me—'

She didn't need him to tell her that, or why. 'The people need you,' she said, stating a simple fact.

'Yes, they do…and I need you.'

She looked at him, wanting those words to echo in her head for ever.

'I want you to stay here with me in Ferranbeaux, Tara.'

She stared into Lucien's strong, dark face and shivered with desire when he seized her arms. He said the words she'd longed to hear, and yet she knew her hopes were fool's gold. 'As your mistress…?' Her lips were dry, her throat was tight; her heart was breaking as she stared up at him.

Lucien stared at her intently and when he spoke again it was in a low, firm tone so there could be no misunderstanding between them. 'When I marry, it will be for the good of my country.'

'And I have no heritage…'

Lucien didn't answer this; he didn't need to. And who was she to question him? He was a warrior who would be her protector. He was the man she adored—should she put a price on love? Lucien was a primal force it took all her mental energy to hold at bay, and he was the ruler of a kingdom who, for now at least, must stand alone.

'I can't…' Her voice barely made it above a whisper. 'I love you more than life itself, but this is the one thing I can't do for you, Lucien…so I'm sorry, but my answer has to be…no.'

CHAPTER THIRTEEN

'WHERE will you go? What will you do? What about Poppy?'

'That all depends on whether you'll sign the lease,' she told him steadily. 'I'll see Poppy every day, of course—nothing will change that.'

He was coming to feel more for Tara than admiration, but it was time to inject some realism into the mix. 'How do you intend to support yourself?'

'I'll work, of course,' she told him, frowning.

When he took in the keen bright gaze he didn't doubt for a moment that she would. Her red-gold hair was still windswept after her adventure, and in spite of the tension of the moment he almost smiled when his gaze landed on the stubborn chin. But it wasn't what he wanted. He wanted to take her tiny feet and warm them in his hands. He wanted to dress her in silk and satin, and see her smile with happiness when he kissed her. He wanted to spoil her and give her the life that she deserved, a life that would take those work-worn hands and make them soft again. He wanted to treat her like a Countess—in all but name.

They had reached an impasse, Tara realised. Lucien

might have started life in poverty and worked his way
up to the very top of the tree, but he had traditional ideas
of a man and woman's role in life. And, though she
relished the thought of him as protector, the thought of
jailer had a different connotation. She couldn't live
where he prescribed in a way he considered appropriate. Even six foot walls, as there were at the castle,
could house a cosy apartment like this one, or those
same walls could become a prison. It all depended on
the people living inside those walls, and the respect, or
lack of it, they felt for each other. Ferranbeaux was
Lucien's home, his sanctuary, and it could be her home
too, if she was allowed to live her life independently, the
way she wanted to.

Lit by firelight and with her hair billowing around her
face like a cloud of gold, he thought Tara the loveliest
woman he had ever seen. She was also, without doubt,
the most aggravating woman on the face of the earth.
Why did she have to make things so difficult for them?
He found himself wishing she had remained the
innocent ingénue, and had to remind himself that he was
largely to blame for the change in her. Who knew what
they were capable of until they were tested? And Tara
had been tested.

He called for warm drinks as they sat on the sofa
talking the tension away deep into the night. He had
asked Tara to tell him more about her childhood. She
made light of it, of course, though the reports he'd read
about it had told him something very different. The
beautiful sister Tara talked about with such love was a
stranger to him, and he could only conclude that much
of Tara's childhood was a fairy tale she had invented to
make it more bearable. He had little admiration for

Freya, but he admired Tara's loyalty towards her sister. The two girls had managed to squeeze more fun out of their miserable early lives than seemed possible, and it was a tribute to both of them. If he could never come to terms with the way Freya had lived her adult life, he did understand Tara's love for her sister a little better now. He even found himself laughing when Tara described some of the innocent scrapes they'd got into. Making the best of things didn't even begin to cover it, he realised, when finally she paused for breath.

'You must miss her,' he said then.

Her eyes filled with tears, which she quickly dashed away with a gulping, 'Sorry…'

'Don't apologise…' Taking out his own clean handkerchief, he handed it to her. 'You should never apologise for showing how much you love someone—'

'Says the expert?' She looked at him ruefully mid-snuffle.

'I'm learning…'

'Thank you for listening—'

'Did I have any choice?' he teased her, leaning forward to flick the curtain of hair from her face so he could kiss the tears away. He felt warmed when she smiled at him, and when she laughed and her hair floated back again he brushed it away and cupped her face. 'I didn't mean to make you cry.'

'I'm not over losing Freya yet… She had such a big personality; she left a big hole—' She touched her chest over her heart and couldn't say any more. She didn't need to. He felt the same way about Guy. His brother might not have had Freya's larger than life personality, but he had left no less of a gap in Lucien's world. He hadn't allowed himself to feel this way since Guy's death, or maybe ever, Lucien realised, but just talking to Tara had freed something inside him.

'Come here,' he said softly, drawing her into his arms.

'Lucien?' Her voice was very small as she looked to him, and at that moment he knew there was nothing he wouldn't do for her.

'Yes?' he said, planting a tender kiss on the top of her head.

'Can I stay with you tonight?'

He should have known her demands on him would be very small.

The promise of Lucien's firm touch made her sob with impatience. The sweet pain was growing inside her, and as he lowered her to the bed she kept hold of him so that he joined her, kissing her deeply, passionately, hungrily, as she moved against him. It was a tender and poignant moment, marking her route to independence as well as heralding her departure from the castle, where she had so briefly enjoyed living with him.

To distract from these unhappy thoughts, she dug her hands down the neck of his open shirt, thrilling at the feel of his back, so smooth and strong. 'You look so severe,' she teased him when he held her away from him to study her face.

'Because there are things I cannot change,' he told her with shadows crossing back and forth behind his eyes.

She understood what he meant, because she felt that way too. But it wasn't long before the great sense of belonging to each other broke through. First they exchanged a look of understanding, and then they were laughing and tearing at each other's clothes. Buttons flew everywhere as she tugged off Lucien's shirt, wrenching it from the waistband of his jeans, while he brought her beneath him with such force the breath shot from her lungs. 'I love you,' she murmured, not even knowing if she had truly spoken or if he had heard.

Gasping with excitement to see Lucien looming above her, Tara gave her wrists readily to be held above her head, while Lucien impatiently pushed up her top.

And now it was Lucien's turn to groan with satisfaction as he gazed at her breasts. She had never been more grateful for the fact that they were nice, big breasts, soft and round, with nipples that strained towards him like brazen lozenges. In the unlikely event he'd missed their appeal she arched her chest towards him, displaying them proudly. 'Do you like them?'

'I love…' Lucien paused as if she had distracted him from some deeper thought. 'I love them,' he confirmed passionately.

Hearing nothing now, she bucked towards him, nipples straining painfully. 'Oh, please…' she cried out with pleasure as Lucien began to suckle and, lacing her fingers through his hair, she kept him close, succumbing to the magic of his hands. 'It isn't fair,' she pointed out. 'You still have your clothes on…'

'You'd better do something about it then, hadn't you?' Lucien suggested with deliberate calm.

She started with the buckle of his belt but, before she had chance to free it, Lucien whipped it off and tossed it onto the floor to join their mounting pile of clothes. It still wasn't enough. She wanted more. She was ravenous to touch him, to taste and feel him. She wanted to feel his hot flesh against her, smooth against rough… His chest was broad and strong, shaded with dark hair, and all of him was deeply tanned.

All of him?

Sucking in a fast breath, she quickly looked away. 'Surely you're not still frightened of me?'

Frightened? Where Lucien was concerned, not at all, it was just the thought of a future without him that frightened her. 'You have no shame,' she said in an attempt to distract herself from these unhappy thoughts.

'Should I, with you?'

Her answer was to fall back on the pillows. 'Make love to me…'

Cupping her face in his hands, Lucien kissed her deeply, making her feel like the most cherished woman on the face of the earth. If tonight was all there was, it would have to be enough.

She'd had the place a week when he stood grimly by while she turned the key in the lock. She had come to the castle every day to spend time with Poppy, while he had signed the lease on what appeared to him now to be a derelict building. The first time he had taken a look, his initial reaction had been to have it condemned and knocked down, until Tara had talked him out of it. She had chosen a simple dwelling in an up-and-coming part of town—more coming than up, as far as he could tell. Her small apartment was located on the fringes of the commercial centre, an area that had attracted some of the smaller artisan cooperatives and boutique businesses. Tara had told him she felt at home here, she would live upstairs and her childcare agency office would open on the ground floor.

Right now, her face was alive with anticipation as she prepared to reveal her Shangri-La, while he was already running a number of rescue scenarios that would allow her to leave all this behind and return to him with her pride intact. 'There are boarded-up windows either side of the property, for goodness' sake,' he commented, thinking of her safety. She didn't even hear him.

'I hope you like what I've done with it—'

Hard for him to answer when he had to snatch out a hand to stop her tripping over the rotten door frame.

'It'll be great when it's all fixed up,' she assured him confidently.

'Better start by fixing that door,' he suggested dryly.

'It's all in hand. I've got a handyman—'

'You've got a what?' He frowned. A muscle worked in his jaw. 'I'll fix it for you.'

'Would you?' she asked him sweetly—so sweetly he wondered if he'd just been set up.

'That's really kind of you, Lucien. I've got some tools—'

His look silenced her.

'Well, we'd best get on,' she said, moving ahead of him up the stairs. 'I know how busy you are.'

He was never too busy for Tara, he had discovered, especially since she'd moved in here.

'And don't worry,' she said, stopping on the stairs to turn to him. 'Clearing the garden out back so Poppy can play outside is a top priority. I'll have it finished long before she starts walking—'

'And Liz? Where will she sleep?'

'If she could stay at the castle for the time being with Poppy—'

He thought how beautiful she looked, how vital, as she continued to explain her vision to him. Her face hadn't changed, but her spirit had grown beyond all imagining since that first strained day at the press conference.

'Honestly, Lucien, it won't take me long to make the place feel like a real home—'

As they came into the large open space at the top of the stairs, he thought Tara's enthusiasm must have got the better of her. Where was she going to find the imagination to turn a rundown room with a naked light bulb into a cosy nest? As far as he could see, there was a kitchen in a cupboard, a bathroom that had seen better days—everywhere he looked the paint was peeling and the tap was leaking. 'Doesn't that thing drive you mad?'

'You could fix that too…maybe…' She looked at him hopefully. 'Seeing as you're here…'

'Perhaps I could,' he admitted grudgingly, looking away before her turquoise eyes could work their magic. Restoration was his passion, but he didn't live on the building site while things were being improved, and he wanted better for Tara. He wanted to sweep her up and install her in the gatehouse this minute, where there was no damp, no draughts, no peeling paint and the latest high-tech plumbing in every bathroom.

'Well? Come on…tell me… What do you think?' Turning full circle, she began to describe her vision. 'I can put the bed here, the table over here—'

'Tara—' he frowned as he interrupted her '—you can't go on living here.'

'Why ever not?'

'Because the whole building should be condemned.'

'Like your basilica?'

He firmed his jaw; she did too.

'When my business expands—'

'Your business?' He had to rein himself in. How could he take this from her when just talking about her plans made her face light up like sunrise?

'My childcare agency,' she reminded him. 'Another signature I need from you, apparently. When are you going to change these antiquated laws, Lucien?'

'When you give me time,' he told her dryly, peeling off some paint that brought a chunk of plaster with it.

'Hey, don't wreck the place—'

His lips tugged up as he stared at her. 'I could knock it down for you, if you like.'

'I don't like. You leave my house alone—'

He had to be content with a mocking smile that made her cheeks pink up.

'When Poppy's older, which hopefully will coincide with my business expansion,' she continued, 'I'm going to turn the whole of the ground floor into business premises. This whole area will be for us then, and she can play here and we'll do baking and—'

'On that cooker…?'

'You'd be surprised what I can do, Lucien—'

He doubted that, somehow.

'And look,' she said.

'Look where?' he said, searching for clues in the dismal room.

'Ta da!' she exclaimed, throwing out her arms in front of a dingy alcove.

'Yes?' His imagination was really flagging now.

'Can't you see?' she demanded. 'This is perfect for my desk. I'll be able to keep an eye on Poppy while I'm working—so much better than London, where I hated having someone looking after her while I had to work.'

'But Poppy will be living with me,' he reminded her.

'But I'll have her to stay here sometimes; she is my niece—'

'So you're going to be working with a small child in the room?'

'Like every other single mother, I'll manage,' she told him confidently.

'But you don't have to manage,' he reminded her patiently. 'And how much money do you think it's going to cost to turn this space into both a functioning office and a home?'

'I've got some savings. I'm not completely destitute.'

'I don't suggest you are, but—'

'But what, Lucien? Oh, I see. You think the niece of the Count of Ferranbeaux couldn't possibly come to stay in a modest apartment in the shadow of your castle.'

'I didn't say that.'

'You didn't have to, and I happen to think it's important to show Poppy the other side of life.'

'The seedy side?'

'The real side, Lucien… The side of life where people have to take decisions and don't have someone standing behind them ready to clear up the mess if they get it wrong. The side of life where you learn to live within your means—'

'You don't have to do that here, you can do it equally well in the gatehouse.'

'Other people want to move to this area,' she insisted, selling it hard, 'and there are families who have stuck it out here for generations. Do you want them to go on living with boarded up windows, because they will if we don't make a start on regenerating the area. Basilicas are important, but so are people—'

'And who do you think will be using the basilica?'

'All right,' she conceded, 'maybe we both need to give a little.'

Wisely, he declined to comment.

'Or maybe you can't bring yourself to admit I can make a go of this.'

'You may have found one solution, but it's not ideal—'

'Can you come up with a better one?'

His mouth curved. 'My gatehouse?'

'By your own admission, Lucien, you started with nothing. Are you denying me the same chance to prove myself? Or are you saying I'm not as good as you?'

Easing onto one hip, he gave her a dark look, and as he stuck his thumbs through the belt loops of his jeans he noticed how she blushed and how her gaze strayed where it shouldn't. He also noticed she had positioned herself in front of a cracked window pane in the hope he wouldn't see it. Perhaps it was that that made up his mind for him. 'Give me a list of what you need—'

'A list?' Her brow puckered attractively.

'Pen, paper—a list? I'm asking what you need to make this work.'

'I'll make this work,' she said quietly, and then her smile broke through. 'You're backing my decision to live here—'

'I'm giving you another week.'

CHAPTER FOURTEEN

THE week before Lucien was due to come and inspect her handiwork passed in a whirl of activity, and one big and wonderful surprise.

'Marian Digby!' Tara exclaimed, opening the door to an old friend from her college days. 'I knew you wouldn't let me down.' Of all the people she had met in the university canteen shared by all the colleges, the eccentric lecturer in historical architecture was one of her very favourite people.

After exchanging hugs and greetings, Marian revealed that she had gone to the castle first. 'I couldn't resist,' she confided, her bright, birdlike eyes twinkling. Lucien had found her wandering in the gardens apparently, and had arranged for his chauffeur to deliver her to Tara's new abode.

'This is wonderful,' Marian commented, wiping her nose on a large duster she had plucked from her pocket, scattering plaster dust as she examined the walls. Realising her old friend probably thought she was using a handkerchief, Tara quickly pressed a tissue into her hand.

'What a wonderful opportunity you've given me,' Marian murmured, without realising the exchange had been made. 'There are so many wonderful old buildings in Ferranbeaux… Isn't this a thirteenth-century siege stone?' she demanded of no one in particular, having forgotten Tara was even there as she wandered distractedly across the room.

'I wouldn't know,' Tara admitted as her friend scrutinised the ancient artefact.

'When you rang to say you had something interesting for me to look at, I had no idea,' Marian exclaimed, switching her keen gaze to Tara's face. 'Don't tell me that you and the Count—'

'Oh, no. No, no, no,' Tara rebuked her friend, whilst trying to adopt a serious expression. 'I wouldn't bring you all this way to offer your expert opinion on the Count—'

'More's the pity,' the older woman twinkled.

He brought a picnic with him for the second visit. He couldn't possibly imagine that things had changed so much that Tara could provide them with lunch.

She lost no time proving him wrong.

'I think you'll see some changes,' she warned him.

'I'll be surprised if I don't,' he told her dryly, following her up the stairs.

Some changes?

What Tara had achieved in her second week, with the help of a few workmen, was nothing short of a miracle. The unpromising space had been transformed. Richly patterned fabrics hung from newly plastered and decorated walls, and there was an attractive light fitting where a naked light bulb had hung. Matching table lamps toned with thick-piled rugs, and the floor was freshly sanded and newly polished. There were comfortable throws flung over the backs of sofas that faced each other across a low table in front of the wide stone hearth, and a gleaming brass fireguard to protect inquisitive children from the flames. The mantelpiece already boasted several photographs of Poppy, and on the sills beneath the tall sash windows an array of healthy looking plants competed for attention alongside examples of colourful local pottery.

'This is lovely,' he said, taken aback.

'I'm glad you like it,' she said with a teasing smile.

Tara had turned a dilapidated space into a home. But where had she found the money? He wondered sometimes if the suspicious gene was part of his genetic make-up. 'How—' He got no further because she knew him too well.

'One person's clutter is another person's treasure. So while I was canvassing opinion about the crèche I'm going to open, I came up with the idea of starting a second-hand stall to help fund it and buy the little extras we're sure to need—'

'A market stall?' He laughed when she nodded enthusiastically. 'I have to hand it to you, Tara Devenish, you're a tycoon in the making.'

'I'm just practical,' she said. 'Don't look so surprised; I wasn't born with a silver spoon in my mouth—'

'Neither was I,' he reminded her.

She had prepared a feast for him, which he had not expected. It made his picnic basket redundant and touched him more than he could say. The tiny kitchen had not expanded, but she had kept everything cool in the lock-up downstairs. She had even baked a cake for him in the tiny table top oven.

'Leave your food with me,' she insisted when he

made some comment about them not eating it, 'and then I'm sure you'll come back again,' she told him shyly.

'I'll come back,' he assured her.

At one time this would have been his cue to lean over and plant a kiss on her mouth, but something had changed. It was like starting over. He wanted to hold onto that feeling and see where it went. He'd underestimated Tara even more than he'd first thought, and he was only now beginning to appreciate the huge mistake he'd made.

'I spoke to your Mrs Digby...'

'Did you like her?' Her eyes twinkled with mischief as they got up and started to clear the dishes.

'She's mad, but brilliant—'

'She's a mad genius.'

'I tend to agree with you on that.'

'Marian's a specialist in Gothic architecture. When they need to consult anyone about Notre Dame in Paris they call Marian Digby. I thought she'd be just the person you need to help you with your restoration of the basilica...'

'You were right, and I thank you.' He'd offered her nothing, he'd treated her badly, and yet still she had been thinking of him all along. As his admiration grew he had to shift position to ease the pressure in his groin. 'I shouldn't have come straight from the basilica—' He slapped his thigh, more to deter this surge of interest than to dislodge any dust he might have collected. 'I apologise for not being more smartly dressed.' He indicated his frayed jeans, cinched with a heavy-duty workman's belt along with his ripped and faded top, which he knew together with his disreputable stubble must make him look more like a pirate than a Count. 'That woman is a demanding taskmaster—'

'I'm sure you'll cope,' Tara told him, pointedly not looking where she shouldn't.

'I'm sure I will,' he agreed. But he didn't want to cope with a groin in torment—he wanted to make love to her.

He admired her on so many fronts—for making a go of this apartment, and perhaps most of all for refusing to lower her standards. They were on heat in each other's company, and it would have been the easiest thing in the world for her to take him up on his offer and move into the gatehouse, where they could sate that passion every day and every night. How could he not respect her for holding firm? How could he not respect the fact that Tara was vulnerable and innocent and beautiful, and more than capable of standing on her own two feet, as she had more than proven here? Plus she was caring and astute…

Had he just drawn up the résumé for a Countess? he wondered and, if he had, had he left it too late?

'So you like the apartment?' she said.

'Now don't put words in my mouth,' he warned her.

She stared at his lips.

'Nothing you could do would surprise me, Tara.'

She put that assumption to the test right away. Reaching up, she locked her fingers behind his neck and, as she drew him down to her, the aquamarine eyes widened. 'How much have you missed me, Lucien?'

It was a situation that didn't call for words. They were alone and they wanted each other; even a day was too long, and it had been more than a week. Buttons flew, zips whirred and belts fell to the floor. He kicked their clothes away as he lifted her. They barely made it to the sofa before they were drowning in liquid desire.

Lucien had her dress up and her briefs down with her legs locked around his waist before she had even time to draw breath. And now she couldn't draw breath—at least, not evenly. If she hadn't needed him… If she hadn't wanted him so badly… If she hadn't loved him so deeply…

'Lucien…' She called his name and clung to him and, as always the only thing that mattered now was this moment.

When she finally quietened Lucien held her safe in the circle of his arms. 'We share a bruising passion,' he murmured.

'Do you think it will ever burn out?'

'I doubt it,' he said with satisfaction, teasing her lips with his teeth and with his tongue.

Reaching out, he laced his fingers through her hair, allowing himself a few moments of self-indulgent pleasure before positioning her.

'Lucien, behave… We should clear up… We've got lots to do.'

'Indeed we have,' he agreed, nudging his way between her thighs again.

'I've missed you,' she confessed in a ragged whisper, locking her arms around him.

'And I've missed you too,' he assured her as he lifted her on top of him to rock her rhythmically.

'I need this,' she gasped out as her excitement mounted.

'We both do,' he assured her huskily. He took her again, firmly, in one long ecstatic thrust. She felt so good, so tight, so warm and lush, better than she ever had. From now on it was Tara's needs all the way. Pleasing her came as naturally as breathing to him and when she called out his name and clung to him fiercely he didn't try to hold her back. He rocked her steadily in his arms until she quietened and when he felt her relax he saw the tears were back again. 'What's this about?' he asked her softly, dropping kisses on her swollen lips.

'I just feel so emotional all the time…'

'You're not pregnant, are you?' He laughed.

'No, don't be silly…' Her cheeks blazed red beneath his kisses.

He willed his strength into her. She had come so far and had achieved so much more than he'd expected, he couldn't bear to see her upset like this. 'Do I make you unhappy?'

'No, of course not,' she told him with a fresh flood of tears.

'Well, what is it, then, *ma petite*?'

'I don't know,' she wailed. 'Just make love to me and forget…'

Forget Tara? Hadn't he tried that before?

As the fire crackled and Lucien made love, Tara knew her common sense was firmly on hold. All those late nights and early mornings sorting out the apartment had been worth it, that was all she knew, and she was exhausted, hence the tears. And this was perfect; this was how it was meant to be. This was everything she had always dreamed a home would be, and with Lucien tending to her every need it was all too easy to take the next step and convince herself this situation would last for ever.

'You are the sexiest man alive,' she murmured in the brief interlude between kisses, 'and I love you…'

A golden haze of contentment surrounded them as they snacked on the food, and kissed and murmured their way through the champagne he'd brought with him. He couldn't imagine anything better than this, or that anything could spoil it.

'That was a contented sigh,' Tara commented.

'I'm happy for you. I'm happy the way things have turned out. The way you've made a life for yourself in Ferranbeaux will—'

'—Make things so much easier for Poppy as she grows up,' she supplied, cutting across him when he had been about to say that Tara living here would allow her to share in the exciting rebirth of a city and would make him happy too.

Always kind words, thoughts and deeds for anyone other than herself, he thought, brushing the hair back from her eyes. He saw the flicker in her eyes that said she would always be hoping for something more from him where their relationship was concerned, but instead of complaints she put her hand over his as if to console him.

'You have to bloom where you're planted, Lucien—' She said this lightly, as if she was resigned to the hand that fate had dealt them, but as a draught of cold air enveloped them she shivered, as if destiny had whispered in her ear.

The gust gave him the opportunity to turn to practical matters he could do something about. 'I must remember to get that window fixed for you.'

'Not now,' she said, cupping his chin to reclaim his attention.

'Not now,' he agreed, holding the lovely turquoise gaze. He was going to make love to her now.

CHAPTER FIFTEEN

SHE had been sick all morning and now she felt dizzy too. Could it be the food she'd fed Lucien? Tara paled until she decided it was time to stop fooling herself. Gripping onto the edge of the sink until she felt safe to move had given her plenty of time to mull over the possibilities. She would have heard from Lucien by now if he was ill and the changes in her body were undeniable. Her breasts felt tender and her emotions were in shreds. She was pregnant with Lucien's baby. A great swell of love and fear hit her concurrently as she stared down at the shiny cold porcelain, willing strength into her shaking limbs.

There was no point panicking; she had to think. Lucien had returned to the castle in the early hours, and she didn't kid herself—this was how it would be from now on. She would remain independent and live here where the Count would visit her—discreetly, of course—and in time people would come to accept their relationship. She would work hard for Ferranbeaux and hopefully prove to be a role model for Poppy in spite of her irregular circumstances.

Once she was feeling steadier, Tara took a shower

and dressed neatly before heading for town. This was too important to take chances, she had to be sure.

It would have been easier to keep her head down and focus on the job in hand if so many people hadn't greeted her along the way. There was an air of purpose in Ferranbeaux and Tara had thrown herself into it, taking on a restoration project of her own as well as planning ahead to provide a useful service with her childcare agency. This can-do attitude had won her a lot of friends in a short time, but now she felt as if she was letting those friends down. Her worst fear was that the people of Ferranbeaux might think she had engineered this pregnancy to snare their Count.

Would Lucien think that? Tara's stomach clenched as the cheery bell over the pharmacy door announced her arrival in the shop. She was greeted warmly by both the assistants and the other customers, but for the first time since coming to Ferranbeaux she felt embarrassed, and unworthy of so much affection. Too many hormones swirling round her body, Tara reasoned, feeling faint again as she approached the discreetly placed pharmacy desk. She stumbled over her request, and then hurried out of the shop to race back home to conduct the test. In spite of her concerns she was excited beyond belief, because this was just about the most wonderful thing that had ever happened to her.

The instructions on the box said that at this early stage of pregnancy she should be able to see a faint response in the test windows. The reaction in the first window would prove the test was working properly, and the second window would show whether or not she was pregnant.

When the test showed a positive result elation battled

with the anxiety inside her. There was only one certainty, which was she loved this baby already. Her child would be a friend for Poppy. Now she had two children to love.

And Lucien? Tara's inner voice prompted. What would he think about this?

The same as everyone else, Tara concluded—that a woman who prided herself on her independence had committed the modern woman's cardinal sin. What was her excuse for this, by the way? But would she change anything? Surely that was the only important question. Knowing the answer to that was a firm and unequivocal no made everything seem brighter. She had always wanted this, Tara reasoned, tracing the outline of her still flat stomach with awestruck hands, and she would handle the practical consequences the same as any other woman. Sluicing her face in cold water, she stared at her glowing reflection in the mirror. Would Lucien guess just by looking at her? She wasn't naïve enough to think the pharmacist might not say something and nothing spread faster than rumour—she must tell him right away.

She almost jumped out of her skin to find Lucien on the doorstep as she left the house.

'I couldn't stay away,' he admitted, trapping her between him and the door jamb, and staring down at her until every inch of her was consumed by desire for him. Her heart was thundering, with anxiety and excitement. She had imagined there would be time to prepare. She had intended walking to the castle and having a plan all sorted out by the time they met.

'Well,' he murmured, making her ear lobe buzz with sensation, 'can I come in?'

No book she had ever read had warned about the pheromones running riot through her body along with the rest of the pregnancy hormones. She was melting, yearning, lusting, and pressing herself quite shamelessly against the marauding pirate in her way. How was she supposed to resist him, when Lucien was dressed in his work clothes of close fitting jeans and a casual top and his sensual face was covered in coarse black stubble?

'Haven't you shaved yet?' she reprimanded him softly.

'Later…'

She swallowed deep, feeling an almost primal desire to claim her mate. 'You'd better come in…'

'You're not too busy to see me, I hope?' he murmured wickedly. Cupping her chin, he brushed her mouth with one of his devastatingly frustrating almost-kisses.

'Too busy?' She shuddered out a moan as he ran his fingertips down her spine.

'Give me the keys,' Lucien whispered, recovering them from her shaking fingers. 'Let's go inside.'

There were people on the street… She should tell him right away… She would, the moment they got inside the house…

They stood facing each other in the main room, Lucien leaning against the table like a sleepy tiger. He said something in his own language. She understood. She might not know the words, but her nipples peaked immediately. Lucien's skill in bed had made her insatiable and now she was focused only on that.

A single step bridged the gap between them. She took it.

Lucien took hold of her, but far too lightly. She moaned, softening against him, while Lucien stared straight into her eyes, telling her he knew she was ready for him.

He loved making her wait. He loved seeing the excitement and anticipation building on her face. He led her by the hand into the bedroom, where he undressed her with studied care. When he had removed the last shred of Tara's clothing he took a moment to appreciate a body that an artist such as Rubens would have fought to paint.

Tara might be young, but she was a proper woman with proper buttocks, and proper thighs to hold him in place. Her generous breasts weighed heavily in his hands, and as he stroked the soft swell of her belly she eased her legs apart and he felt the heat of her.

It must be the pregnancy, Tara thought wildly; she had never been so responsive to Lucien's touch. She should tell him now…right away…

One more time, and then she'd tell him…

Exhaling raggedly as Lucien ran his warm palms down her neck to her breasts, which he cupped, she swayed against him. One more time…

She thrashed her head about on the pillows as he worked steadily with concentrated intent to satisfy her ravenous demands. Would she ever get enough of this—of him? He had taken her slowly and carefully, the way she had always liked before, but today was different, she had been almost frantic for release though it was only hours since they had last been together. She called out to him now, holding herself as if she wanted to isolate the source of her pleasure and concentrate only on that, while he grasped her buttocks in his work-roughened hands and rocked her beneath him in a prolonged assault that no sooner resulted in a sustained firestorm of pleasure than the next build-up began. It was several hours before he felt a new ease in her and, feeling it, he withdrew carefully and, wrapping her in his arms, he watched her sleep.

When he was confident she was sleeping soundly and he wouldn't disturb her, he left her side to take a shower. Towelling down afterwards, he happened to glance across at the shelf where she kept her make-up and suddenly everything made sense. She had tasted different—sweeter, fuller, richer. She even looked different—there was a glow about her. Clutching the cold, unyielding sink he stared into the mirror. He was ecstatic at the thought that Tara was carrying his child, but concerned that she had excluded him. The sense of being shut out had dogged him since childhood when his father the Count had not wanted his illegitimate son cluttering up the picture, let alone distracting his mistress from her main responsibility, which the Count had considered to be him. A shudder of resentment ran through him at the thought that history was repeating itself, only now Tara was denying him the chance of loving his own child.

'Why didn't you tell me?'

'Mmm…?' Tara's eyelids fluttered as she moved slowly from sleep to full consciousness. All that activity had left her very groggy, but somewhere down the end of a very long tunnel she knew that Lucien was talking to her. His voice sharpened as he asked the question again, and this time she woke up to find him resting on one elbow on the bed, staring down at her.

He knew.

Her stomach was in knots as she struggled to read every nuance in his stern face.

'Why didn't you tell me about the baby? I thought you trusted me, Tara—'

'I do trust you—'

'So you trust me enough to sleep with me, but not to tell me about the single most important change in your life?'

'I only just found out.'

'When were you going to tell me? Oh, I see,' he exclaimed tensely before she had a chance to answer. 'After I slept with you.'

'Don't say it like that. You make me feel so—'

'Cheap?'

'Lucien, please—' When she tried to touch him he shook her off. 'I won't embarrass you. I'll leave Ferranbeaux—'

'What are you saying, Tara? What about Poppy?'

She shivered as the full extent of her foolishness came home to her. 'I'd never leave Poppy. I was half asleep... I wasn't thinking straight.'

'If you think I'd let you leave Ferranbeaux while you're carrying my baby, you aren't thinking straight,' Lucien agreed. Seizing hold of her wrists, he brought her in front of him.

'Lucien, no... Surely, you can't believe I would do that?' It was so far from the truth, it made her feel sick.

'Why are you denying me the right to know about my child, then?' he said, staring intently at her. 'Did you think I wouldn't sleep with you if you told me? Did you think I'd walk out on you? What?' he demanded angrily.

Colour drained from Tara's face. How could she tell Lucien the truth—that she loved him so much she would do anything to protect him from reliving the shame that had scarred him as a boy, only this time through their innocent baby?

'If you feel so cheap after sleeping with me,' Lucien

spat out with contempt, 'perhaps I should go...' Swinging off the bed, he snatched up his clothes.

'Don't leave like this,' she begged him, dragging a sheet around her so she could chase him to the door. 'I won't cause you any trouble... I'll get a lawyer... I'll sort this out.'

'Sort what out?' Lucien demanded, slowly turning to face her.

'My rights...your rights...the baby...'

'Your rights to my money...?'

'Of course not,' Tara exclaimed in absolute horror.

'Then let's get one thing straight,' he said. 'Poppy isn't leaving here, and neither are you.'

But it was all too much for her in her present state, and as Lucien rapped this last command at her she almost fainted. Brought up short, he caught her to him. 'I can't believe this is happening...' Her voice was muffled in his chest, but in spite of his concern Lucien felt stiff and unresponsive.

'You regret the fact that you are pregnant?' Lucien rapped.

'No, of course I don't—'

'What, then?'

'I just feel—'

'Yes?'

'Foolish,' she admitted softly. 'With all my talk of independence and standing on my own two feet...' It was Tara's turn to stiffen with surprise when she felt Lucien's hold on her soften.

'Perhaps I'm a little more experienced than you,' he suggested with formidable understatement, 'but, as far as I recall, it takes two to make a baby.'

'So you're not angry with me?'

'I'm angry that you didn't tell me, but angry about your news? No. How could I be, when it's the most wonderful news I've ever heard?'

'And you're not embarrassed?'

'That I've fathered a child?' Lucien gave a short and very masculine laugh. 'It would take a lot more than your pregnancy to embarrass me, and the gatehouse will make the perfect family home for you and my baby.'

Tara froze. She should have known Lucien's reaction was too good to be true, and now who was making history repeat itself? 'I won't live there,' she said flatly.

'What do you mean?' Lucien was still in magnanimous mode and had yet to pick up on the fact that she was utterly serious.

'This is my home now...' She glanced around before walking back to the bed where she curled up, hugging a pillow.

'It's not good enough—'

For an aristocratic baby? She let Lucien's words hang for a moment, and then sat up. 'Don't you mean I'm not good enough?'

He frowned.

She discarded the pillow and got up. 'My expectations in life are very different from yours, Lucien. You have a sense of entitlement that I lack, plus you have everything rigidly sorted out in your head. I just want to be happy with the people I love. I want to be a good mother to Poppy and our baby, and to remain in Ferranbeaux, where I can work on the regeneration of the city with everyone else. I don't care about position or wealth or any of that. I just want a family...'

'A family,' Lucien murmured, as if she had mentioned the Holy Grail.

'Yes,' Tara confirmed softly and, sensing she might have landed on the one thing that could reach him she waited a few more moments and then, crossing the room to him, touched his face. 'All I want is a family—a family that's part of a wider family in a country that cares.'

He covered his eyes to hide his emotion as his anger drained away. He didn't deserve her. Tara was too good for him. She was painfully honest and far too capable to need the all-powerful Count to take care of his mistress and their baby. She had proved she could manage perfectly well on her own without him, which stung his male pride. But together…what a force they'd be then!

How wrong he'd been about the meaning of duty. He had thought his country needed a model wife, when what both he and his country needed was a woman who loved his people as much as he did, and who wasn't afraid to get her hands dirty. If his intention was to modernise Ferranbeaux, then the woman at his side must be a thoroughly modern wife. Even more than that, for all their sakes, she must be the woman who had softened him and taught him how to love.

He'd never been impulsive in his life, and it would be irresponsible of him to start now, but Tara had changed everything around him—she had changed his life, making him feel like a youth again, shining light into all the shadows.

'Will you marry me?' he said, driven by these imperative thoughts.

Her brow puckered as she stared at him in confusion.

'Will you marry me, Tara? Will you do me the honour of becoming my wife?'

'Are you serious, Lucien? Lucien, don't tease me,'

she warned him, turning her face away as if she was frightened of what she might see in his.

'If I had to choose a mother for my child, you would be that mother, is that clear enough for you?'

'So you're not angry with me?' she said, turning to him hesitantly.

'Is it usual for a man to be angry when he proposes marriage?'

'I don't know…' She shook her head, looking doubly bewildered. 'I've never been proposed to before—'

'Then let me reassure you…' He took her hand and brought it to his lips.

'You're sure you're not making allowances for my being pregnant?'

'You think I'd go this far?' Lucien's eyes over the back of his hand were black and wicked.

'I wouldn't put too much past you,' Tara said frankly.

'I might make allowances for you being a woman—' he held up his hands in mock surrender when she would have shouted him down, and added softly '—and hormonal, and pregnant. But would I propose marriage?' His lips pressed down. 'Oh, Tara—' his face broke into a smile '—don't you know me at all?'

She'd seen flashes of this new, relaxed Lucien, but memories of the cold, forbidding Count still haunted her. 'I want to believe,' she murmured, voicing her thoughts out loud.

'That I love you?'

She stared at him.

'You can't still be that lost little girl who believes she isn't deserving of love,' Lucien protested, 'or all my efforts have been wasted.' His lips tugged up in an irresistible smile. 'Tell me you believe in love now?'

'I do…'

'In my love,' he insisted.

'In your love…'

'For you,' Lucien prompted. 'Don't you recognise a man who adores you?'

'You…love me?'

'That's not a word I'd choose,' Lucien argued, framing Tara's face with his hands. 'I prefer the word I just used, which I believe was *Je t'adore*. I adore you, *ma petite*…'

CHAPTER SIXTEEN

'WHAT will everyone in Ferranbeaux think if you marry me?' Tara was still not quite ready to believe Lucien had asked her to become his Countess.

'Those we care about will be happy for us; does anyone else matter?'

'The journalists should be happy,' Tara agreed. 'Think how much copy they'll sell. But what about your duty to Ferranbeaux?' she added, frowning.

'What about yours?'

'I would never come between you and your people, Lucien—'

'And I would never ask you to. Is that a yes to my proposal?'

She studied him for a long moment. 'Yes…yes, it is. I will marry you, and I'll do everything in my power to serve the people of Ferranbeaux—'

Lucien greeted this announcement by tumbling her on the bed. 'My people love you already because of the way you have involved yourself in the city, and now it just remains for you to stay on and serve their Count—' His lips tugged up wickedly.

'I could do all that without you having to marry me,'

Tara pointed out, not struggling too hard when Lucien pinned her beneath him.

'I know I shouldn't tease you,' he admitted, brushing frustrating little kisses on her neck, 'especially now, when your head is full of hormones, but you make it so hard to resist...' His eyes glowed with passion as he moved up the bed. 'I want you,' he murmured, staring deep into Tara's eyes, 'and I can't wait. I can't wait for our baby to be born. I want Poppy and the baby and you more than I can possibly tell you...'

But he could show her, Tara thought, making a token push at the wide spread of Lucien's chest. 'You don't play fair,' she complained when he worked his magic on her.

'True,' he agreed, moulding her naked breasts with his work-roughened hands. 'But do you want me to?'

'Yes...no...don't stop...' Pleasure raged between her legs as he teased the tender tip of each nipple in turn. Her thighs were trembling by the time she locked them round his waist.

'Don't worry, I'll be careful,' he assured her, the love in his eyes telling her everything she wanted to know.

'It's a little too late for that.' She exchanged a mischievous look with him.

'And aren't you glad?' he murmured.

Her answer was to strain towards him, but as always Lucien made her wait...a few seconds at most, thankfully, and the hunger in his eyes matched her own.

'This is where you belong,' Lucien told her when she quietened. 'At my side in Ferranbeaux...'

'We'll have to get out of bed occasionally,' she teased.

'Occasionally,' Lucien agreed reluctantly. He kissed the very sensitive nape of her neck, her eyelids and finally her mouth. 'Stay and help me to change things, Tara. I want us to be married very soon.'

Tara's expression grew serious as she considered this; she was still concerned for him. 'Are you sure you don't have to marry someone special?'

'Forgive me,' Lucien murmured, 'but I thought that was exactly what I plan to do.'

EPILOGUE

THE most fabulous wedding Ferranbeaux had ever seen was held in the newly renovated basilica. The marriage of Count Lucien Maxime of Ferranbeaux to the much younger and very pregnant Tara Devenish caused such a stir, but the bride and groom were too much in love to notice the interest they caused. Tara had changed a great deal in the intervening months and walked confidently down the aisle on her own to meet her groom, though perhaps the greatest change of all was in Count Lucien Maxime of Ferranbeaux, whose stern face was transformed when he turned to see his beautiful bride.

There were so many smiling faces waiting to greet the bride and groom when the service was over, and first of these was their newly adopted baby daughter, Poppy, whom Tara carried so that when they went outside the crowds could get a good view of the happy family. Even Marian Digby had exchanged her customary dusty outfit for a smart suit topped off with an extravagantly feathered hat. It was Marian who was ready with Tara's second wedding bouquet of the day, the first having been left that morning at a newly constructed memorial to Freya and Guy. This second bouquet was all the dearer to Tara's heart for being composed of simple flowers picked for their new Countess by the people of Ferranbeaux from their own gardens.

Lucien had indulged Tara in this, because she believed so strongly that they must only talk about Freya with love in front of Poppy. It had taken Tara some time to persuade Lucien to think better of her sister, but when she said that all Freya had really wanted was a home she had struck a chord with him. 'We're so lucky,' she'd pointed out. 'We've got each other, we've got a home for our family—for Poppy *and* the new baby…'

The rest did not need to be said; they had both lost people they loved, and Count Maxime was so deeply in love with his young bride he had chosen not to disagree.

Tara stood modestly on the steps of the basilica at Lucien's side in the gown he had insisted on buying for her in Paris. The world's press took their photographs, which the Count had made them pay dearly for to swell the funds of his beloved wife's newly founded charities. Composed of three types of Swiss lace, the elegant dress Tara had chosen for this special day was decorated with seed pearls and diamanté, and her filmy veil was sprinkled with tiny jewels that twinkled in the sunlight as it lifted in the soft summer breeze. Poppy crowed with contentment in Tara's arms as Tara reflected on a service she had devised with Lucien. Even the sternest face had softened when they'd exchanged their vows, and many of the women were weeping. No one could remember such a moving occasion, many would say later, for neither the Count nor his young bride had forgotten the tragedy that had brought them together.

When they emerged from the basilica into the brilliant sunshine a great cheer went up and it seemed to

Lucien that every citizen in Ferranbeaux had crowded into the square to wish them well. He gazed down with pride at the woman who had changed his life. The woman for whom he had decided that only a clear corn-flower sapphire as blue as Tara's eyes and as pure as her heart should grace her wedding finger. And that night would see them, not on some glamorous yacht, or foreign beach, but at home in the castle of Ferranbeaux, which they now referred to fondly as Castle Cosy since Tara had worked her magic on it for her family.

'I'm the luckiest man alive,' Lucien murmured into Tara's ear.

'And I'm the luckiest woman in the world,' Tara replied, gazing with love at Lucien and then at Poppy.

'To the family,' Lucien said and, as the people of Ferranbeaux applauded, he first kissed Poppy and then, in a manner that set the world's press alight, Tara, one of the notorious Devenish sisters, who was now not only a Countess, but Lucien Maxime's beautiful pregnant wife.

Can this man of duty risk his heart?

Keegan McKettrick has learned the hard way that women can't be trusted. And then beautiful but mysterious Molly Shields arrives on a mission…

Molly doesn't know why she's attracted to a man who's determined to dig up dirt on her, even if he *is* gorgeous.

But cynical Keegan might be the one person who can truly understand her shadowy past…

Available 16th January 2009

www.millsandboon.co.uk

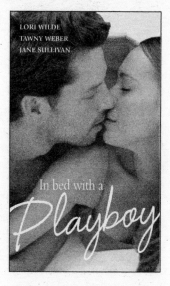

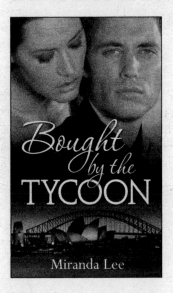

He's her boss in the boardroom – and in the bedroom!

Her Mediterranean Boss
Three fiery Latin bosses
Three perfect assistants
Available 20th February 2009

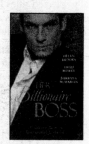

Her Billionaire Boss
Three ruthless billionaire bosses
Three perfect assistants
Available 20th March 2009

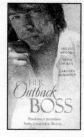

Her Outback Boss
Three sexy Australian bosses
Three perfect assistants
Available 17th April 2009

Her Playboy Boss
Three gorgeous playboy bosses
Three perfect assistants
Available 15th May 2009

Collect all four!

www.millsandboon.co.uk M&B™

FREE

4 BOOKS AND A SURPRISE GIFT!

We would like to take this opportunity to thank you for reading this Mills & Boon® book by offering you the chance to take FOUR more specially selected titles from the Modern™ series absolutely FREE! We're also making this offer to introduce you to the benefits of the Mills & Boon® Book Club™—

- ★ **FREE home delivery**
- ★ **FREE gifts and competitions**
- ★ **FREE monthly Newsletter**
- ★ **Books available before they're in the shops**
- ★ **Exclusive Mills & Boon Book Club offers**

Accepting these FREE books and gift places you under no obligation to buy; you may cancel at any time, even after receiving your free shipment. Simply complete your details below and return the entire page to the address below. You don't even need a stamp!

YES! Please send me 4 free Modern books and a surprise gift. I understand that unless you hear from me, I will receive 6 superb new titles every month for just £2.99 each, postage and packing free. I am under no obligation to purchase any books and may cancel my subscription at any time. The free books and gift will be mine to keep in any case.

P9ZEE

Ms/Mrs/Miss/Mr......................................Initials ....
BLOCK CAPITALS PLEASE

Surname ....

Address ....

....

....Postcode ....

Send this whole page to:
The Mills & Boon Book Club, FREEPOST CN81, Croydon, CR9 3WZ